Books by Bill Thesken

The Lords of Xibalba
The Oil Eater
Blocking Paris
Edge of the Pit

The Catalina Cabal

Bill Thesken

Book cover designed by Deranged Doctor Design

Edited by Jilly Pretzel

ISBN 978-0-9903519-7-9
E-Book ISBN 978-0-9903519-8-6

"For nothing is secret that will not be revealed, nor anything hidden that will not be known and come to light"

(Luke 8:17)

"His eyes are on the ways of mortals; he sees their every step.
There is no deep shadow, no utter darkness, where evildoers can hide."

(Job 34:21-22)

Cabal:

A group of people working
together in a secret plot.

1.

The trip to the island was mostly uneventful, the winds in the middle of the channel just as I predicted were gusting twenty knots, the seas running eight feet, breaking over the bow like angry white haystacks, and Cody Markender only got swept overboard twice.

The first time was his fault, as he got blindsided by a haystack crashing over the bow while he was tightening up the deck line to the jib sail. I warned him before we got under way: keep one eye on the bow and brace yourself hard when a big one breaks over it. Don't lose focus, I warned him, it's dangerous on deck when we're at sea.

Being a tough, smart kid who knew it all, he just nodded his head with a bit of a smirk and said something like, 'I got this'.

What he got was a butt whupping over the side, nearly conking his head on the deck as he went over, and then dragged by his safety line like shark bait in the wake of the sailboat until I could set the bow into the wind and slow the boat down enough so we could pull him in.

The second time was mostly my fault, and I did it on purpose.

We were pinched hard into the wind, taking a steady northwest tack towards Catalina, looming in the distance two miles away and closing. Six of us on board the 'Sugar': myself and my fiancé Amber, Gale and Cody and their two friends Garrett and Rhonda. I told Cody to go forward on the deck and winch the jib tighter. We were flying over the water but I wanted to go faster.

Since he'd already been swept overboard once just over an hour ago, and nearly died, Cody was a little more cautious this time. But not cautious enough for me.

Not by a long shot.

I told myself at the beginning of this sailing trip to Catalina that I'd teach him how to be on his toes for the unexpected. Train him to be alert and ready for anything. He was one of the main guys that was going to be taking care of Gale after all, and he had to be ready for anything. Her bodyguards weren't always going be nearby and he had to be sharp and on the ball. This was a team effort.

My old man used to rough me up all the time, said it was good for a boy to get jostled around, that it gave him some character and got him ready for the real world. So he started wrestling me from an early age, in fact I couldn't remember a time when he didn't wrestle me, he probably wrestled me out of the womb on the day I was born. And as I got older the roughing up got rougher. He never really hurt me too bad, he'd just jump out at me from odd places, pin me to the ground until I could barely breathe and my bones felt like they were about to break in half, then he'd hug me and set me free and I'd scamper away. I learned to approach doorways and bushes with caution, and to this day even with him long gone I can see him leaping out of the dark at me and pinning my arms behind my head.

I would complain and tell him it wasn't fair.

"Look how big you are, and how small I am."

He'd just laugh and bellow out. "Get big, get strong!" And then tackle me again and pin me on the ground.

One time when I was about eight years old I was taking out the garbage at night, and as a precaution I double checked, peering around the corner from the kitchen. I saw him sitting on a chair, quietly reading a book by a light in the living room. I assumed that it was safe so I took my time meandering out to the side of the yard, petted our cat, watched a moth fly around the lamp-post at the street corner, looked up at the night sky and the stars. When I finally got to the bin he jumped right out of the trash can, the metal lid flew up suddenly and split my upper lip, drops of blood flying in the air, and he still came at me and pinned me on the cement with the garbage bag on my head. I thought it was a normal way for a father to treat his son.

Cody wasn't a small boy, he wasn't my son, and I had only just met him that morning before setting sail, but I still felt responsible for him mostly because he was Gale's boyfriend.

Boyfriend.

I gritted my teeth as I looked at him. Surely she could have picked someone tougher than this guy. What was she thinking? I narrowed my eyes as I watched him walk casually forward towards the winch. Single digit body fat, rail thin, wispy little peach fuzz beard on the tip of his chin. I bet a gust of wind could knock him off the deck as sure as a frothy wave over the bow.

He was getting soft again, losing focus. I could tell by his body language, the lazy languid way his arms and legs flopped at odd angles like limp spaghetti noodles keeping him in balance on the deck as he shuffled forward with a silly grin on his face.

Being on a sailboat can lull you to sleep with the steady rocking and rolling of the hull, the sound of the ocean spray all around you while keeping your eyes on the sails and the ever-moving water. The horizon is mesmerizing and can put you in a trance.

Kind of like life in a way. You get lulled by the ambiance of your surroundings and that's when you let your guard down and put yourself and those around you in danger. My motto is never assume anything, and above all never *ever* assume that everything is going to be 'A-Okay'.

Now he was bracing himself nicely on the deck, keeping one eye on his footing and the other on the bow heading into the swells. I nodded in approval, he was learning.

And then as he crouched down to winch the sail tighter, he took his eye off the bow for a split second to concentrate on the winch that seemed to be stuck. Exactly what I told him not to do. Don't take your eyes off the bow.

Bad move.

I cranked the wheel just a bit to the left. The hull groaned as the bow lurched sideways into a frothing haystack that crashed sideways over the front of the boat and swept him overboard again. Only this time the safety harness line snapped with a loud crack and flew back onto the boat.

Big trouble. Lucky thing I'd trained for this.

"Man overboard!" I yelled, and looked back at Cody flailing his arms to keep his head above the churning water.

I reached to the side, yanked the round orange float from the railing, flew it into the wake behind the boat, and prepared to turn around. You can get lost pretty quick out on the open ocean, there's no landmarks, nothing stable to fix your position on, just endless blue water and whitecaps, and it would take a big round turn to get back to where he fell in. If we lost track of where he was, we'd never find him, he'd be lost for good. The float was as much to mark the spot for us to see, as it was for him to climb into, if he could.

"Hold on!" I yelled at the others, who were stunned to silence, their faces whiter than the sails, as I cranked the wheel and pulled the boat into a jibe stop, which is like a big round circle, first going straight downwind and then heading back upwind to our man overboard.

Maneuvering a sailboat is a lot harder than a power boat, you can't just slow down or stop the engine, back up and circle at will when you're at full sail. You have to use the wind and the jibe would be at least two hundred yards wide, the length of two football fields by the time it was finished. The jib would have to stay winched tight and I loosened the mainsail as we came about to swing our backside around.

"Keep your eyes on him!" I yelled to the others. I concentrated on the wind in the sail, and the open ocean swells barreling down on us, and I turned hard right before a big one that was feathering on the top and rode down into the valley in front of the crest. We were going straight downwind and down swell and the sail would have to flip to the other side.

"Watch your heads!" I yelled at my crew. "Duck down, now!" When I could see they were clear I completed the quarter turn and cranked hard on the wheel. The sail snapped as it caught the wind again from the opposite side, bringing it tight, and we were headed back the way we had come.

I'd have to pass below the spot where he was and then continue the turn and use the boat's momentum to glide to where we could get him on board again. I could see him hanging onto the round orange float about a hundred yards to the right, starboard side. I completed the turn leaning hard on the wheel, we were heading dead into the wind going about two knots with the sails fluttering softly. I brought the bow of the boat just downwind of Cody and as he slid by the side of the boat, I reached down and grabbed tight on both his hands and pulled him up onto the rail.

He sat there gasping for air, still hanging tight to the float, with his legs dangling over the side. His girlfriend Gale Nighting threw her arms around him, she was nearly in tears, hugging and kissing him all over his head and cheeks.

That's when we saw the ten foot long grey shark pass underneath the boat, swimming slow and methodical, heading on the same track as us and just beneath the surface, the tip of its fin tracking through the water. It turned slightly on its side and we could see its shiny black eye look up at us, then swam down and away into the azure blue ocean and disappeared into the depths.

My whole crew was leaning over the side looking at the shark and I didn't want Garrett to miss out on the fun, so I reached over behind his back, grabbed his shoulder and gave him a little shove while grunting in a low voice, "Uhhggg."

He nearly jumped out his skin backwards into the boat, then whispered hoarsely since his voice had disappeared. "Dude, what the heck is wrong with you?" His eyes were the size of dinner plates.

I just chuckled and shook my head. "You city folks are funny, you need to lighten up a little bit. It's just a little shark. Don't worry, I wasn't going to let go of you." These two tough guys wouldn't last five seconds with my Dad. He'd have them bawling their eyes out in no time. I was being easy on them.

"Did you see the size of that thing?" asked Amber. "It was as long as a car."

"I don't think it's a good idea to jump in the water anymore Cody," I said. "Maybe you better stay on the boat until we get to Catalina, what do you say?"

He looked at me with his wisecracker eyes back in full force, and retorted. "Really? Ya think so?"

Then he started coughing again and got slowly to his knees and moved into the interior of the yacht, holding on with both hands and both feet like a crab on the rocks the whole time watching me in the corner of his eyes. With each movement at least three appendages were in direct contact with a solid surface. It looked like he was trying to dig each finger and toe into the fiberglass deck.

It brought a smile to my face. Now you're getting it, I thought.

"You don't have to worry about the deck winch anymore," I said. "It's got an electric drive and I can control it from here."

I pointed to a bank of switches on the side of the wheel housing. His face went blank for a moment and turned bright red, his jaw went slack, and it looked like he wanted to take a swing at me. I got ready to block a punch and then as he saw that everyone was quietly laughing. He shrugged his shoulders in resignation and began to laugh with them.

I felt bad, so I sat next to him and told him a story. "My Dad brought me on a sailboat when I was a kid, and rolled me off a couple of times too, so you're not alone. You either get used to it and take it in the chops, or make sure it doesn't happen again."

"So that explains it."

"And I did it for your own good, just like he did for me. I'll tell you a story my Dad told me after pulling me out of the water one day. He said, life is kind of like a sailboat, son. It's a whole lot easier when your feet are set firmly on the deck. People and events, like the wind and the waves are going to jostle you around and try to knock you off your boat, and strive as you might to keep your feet set firm, they might succeed from time to time and knock you overboard. That's life. But it's always nice to get back on your ship and set your feet solid again and sail on to a new adventure. And, having a helping hand to get you back on board is always a good thing."

I reached my hand out and Cody nodded and shook it.

"Thanks." He said and hesitated for a moment, then added. "Dad." And we all laughed again, satisfied that all was well, I set the sail into the wind.

It took a total of five hours and fifteen minutes to sail from Dana Point to Catalina. The chart showed that it was twenty three miles from port to port so we'd averaged a little more than four knots per hour. Soon, the forty-five foot ketch was settled nicely at her mooring in the middle of the bay and we were safe on land at a noisy bar in the middle of town.

I took a sip of the club soda with lime and took in the view. The back of my chair was set against a stucco wall on the veranda of the bar with a wide view of the bay which was near capacity, the water a hard cobalt blue. Boats of every size and shape were spread out evenly in concentric circles with the largest boats towards the open ocean and the smallest near the beach.

The Sugar was nestled in the third row from the exit to the ocean, next to a fifty-foot ketch on her right and a sixty-foot power boat on her left. In the next row out towards the ocean was an eighty-five-foot black catamaran that looked like it could do some serious knots on the water.

The mast looked like it was nearly a hundred feet tall. Set on top the mast was a giant black pirate flag, the skull and crossbones waving in the on-shore breeze.

Some rich guy's fun toy.

It was a busy day on the island, bustling even some might say for the usually placid town. It was a weekend and there was a huge party that night, a wedding for one the big shots who had a house on the island, a movie producer in Hollywood. Three hundred people were invited, and the event was at the old Zane Grey estate on top of a knoll that looked out over the crystal blue water bay.

Zane Grey's old estate was the perfect place

for the party, it was large enough to accommodate a good sized crowd, had a pool, and a nice view of the Avalon harbor. Plus, it had a bit of history with the island.

Zane's first occupation was as a dentist, but he had a passion for writing, and became one of the best-selling authors of the late nineteen twenties, best known for his westerns, and the book *Riders of the Purple Sage*. He was also a Hollywood player as well, and wrote a couple screenplays for the big screen. Zane's parties were known to rage through the night and the owners of the island, the Wrigley's, were not too pleased. They were not big partiers but were nevertheless impacted by the noise. They eventually placed large wind chimes around the property next door, which would awaken the hungover Zane.

The house had twenty bedrooms and twenty bathrooms and for a period of time was utilized as a hotel, but in later years was abandoned and fell into disrepair until it was sold.

I was there in an official capacity as the perimeter security for Gale Nighting, the one and only Nightingale, top of the pop charts singer and survivor of kidnapping by her wanna-be rap star billionaire boyfriend a year ago. She had recovered nicely from the trauma of being held and nearly killed by that maniac, and since I was the one who lost her, and then saved her, she was doing me the honor of protecting her again. It was a feather in my cap so to speak. It was more of a ceremonial gig since Catalina was known as a safe enclave, far from the blistering asphalt and crime of Los Angeles. Still, anytime you advertised to the world that you would be in a certain place at a certain time, it was a good idea to put out a perimeter. She had two full time bodyguards who had taken a small private helicopter flight over from L.A. and met us on the island.

Kali Moniz, who was with Gale, Rhonda, and Amber, were in the hotel room as Gale got ready for her gig. Tony Piper was sitting with me and Cody and Parker at the bar.

Tony was a tough guy: smart, quick on his feet, ex-Army Ranger and military security in his younger days.

Now, military security can mean a lot of different things, you could be the guy with a rifle standing guard at a door, or the guy making sure that a computer wasn't being getting hacked, or phone lines weren't being bugged. Tony was the guy with the gun.

At one time he was on the staff of the commanding General of NATO, but got caught up in a political snafu, and was asked to retire when the married General that he was protecting got caught fooling around with one of the native housekeepers.

Now in his mid-thirties he was living the good life travelling the world first class with a bona fide star. Gale was his second client after retiring from the military. The first was an infamous rock and roll guitar player from England who liked to get out and party, and needed someone to get him out of trouble most nights. He liked to get drunk and start a fight and then lean on Tony to save him. That got old fast and Tony went looking for a client who was better behaved.

I interviewed him with Gale, and she hired him on the spot. When I shook his hand to congratulate him, it felt like I was shaking hands with an anvil.

"You know Badger," he told me. "Rock stars and generals are a lot alike, they love the power and the attention and love to be on stage and be in control, but when they get in trouble they look for someone else to save them."

I admired him, he was a no-nonsense guy and I knew Gale would be in good hands with him in charge of her security. But he had one fatal flaw as far as I was concerned.

"I don't like boats," he said while we planned the trip last week. "Toss me out of a plane with or without a parachute, or let me rappel out of a helicopter into an enemy machine gun nest at night in the rain, but keep me away from boats, I get seasick just looking at them." And apparently from what I'd heard, Cody had scoffed at that. A big tough Army Ranger afraid of a little bitty boat.

Now however, after being dragged behind my boat like a tuna on a line, Cody's tune had changed. "I'm taking the flight back with you," he told Tony flat out as he sipped his beer.

I stirred the club soda on ice and smiled. "You all are. Amber and I are staying on the island for a couple of days to unwind."

"Now you're talking," laughed Cody. "No offense Badger, but I don't think I'm a boat guy either."

"No skin off my knuckles."

"We had a change of plans," said Tony. "Gale needs to be in Los Angeles early tomorrow morning for an interview, so we're leaving tonight after the party. I kept our chartered helicopter here, we leave at seven tonight after her gig."

Cody smiled and let out a sigh of relief.

I took another sip of the club soda and got down to business. "Listen Tony, it's about an hour until you head up the hill with Gale. I think it's best for me to go in ahead of you to check the edges of the place and get a feel for it. But let's talk security for a bit if you don't mind. I'm just curious how you're doing."

"Fire away." He shrugged, thinking better of that as he noted the bulge of the gun inside my jacket. "I mean fire away with questions."

"I don't want to get too inquisitive with all the little details of your operation, I just want to get an overall feel for how you're coping as a team. Having a security firm protecting you is like being on a football or baseball team: you all have to work together and be on the same page to be successful and stay out of trouble. To stay in one piece. To stay alive. Since I'm connected to Gale in a way, I'm just wondering how she's doing overall with your set-up?"

"She's okay. As you're well aware, it's been about half a year since she was kidnapped and you rescued her, and I don't think the trauma of that experience will ever completely leave her. Nor should it. She's coming to the realization that she'll never be completely and totally safe in this world and she's made adjustments both mental and physical to enable her to live a solid life. She's a big star now, it's her choice, she could have crawled under a rock and gone underground, but she's out there in the public eye and there's always going be some wacko lurking in the shadows. But she's determined not to be a victim, and I don't think she'll ever allow herself to be taken again. No way. She doesn't want us hovering around her at her home when she's not touring. Sure, we have the perimeter secured and monitored at all times, but we're nowhere near the main house. When she's out on tour we're close by, on-stage and in the dressing areas. When she's out in public, out on the town or in a crowd situation, we're right there at her elbow. Otherwise she wants space, she needs space to be secure in her own mind with her own ability to protect herself, and that has been a key to her recovery. It's been empowering to her and it's good to see."

"What's her training like, and what type of personal protection does she carry?"

"Well, she's learning a few different martial arts. Karate, Jujitsu, Krav Maga. She carries triple action pepper spray with mace and a marking dye, and a little Glock G-42 subcompact. It's six inches long and an inch wide and she can carry it in her purse or holster it. It's small and indiscreet, and while it doesn't have a lot of long distance stopping power, if someone is up close and trying to harm her, they won't last long."

"What about a little hand held taser? I've always had great luck with those, saved my butt a few times. You can incapacitate someone quicker with one of those than a bullet."

"She's afraid of the electricity. We tried one out, a little palm sized one, and she wanted to see what it was like to get zapped, so she went ahead and zapped herself and, of course, fell on the ground and was unable to move for a couple of minutes. She didn't like the thought of accidently jolting herself into paralysis. She feels she has it covered with the spray and the gun and the martial arts, and I don't want to argue with her."

"I've got the taser part covered," said Cody with a sly smile, and reached into his pocket and pulled out a little black object that looked like a cell phone. It was square and fit in the palm of his hand, with two metal prongs at one end and he pressed a switch on the side and a blue electric current crackled loudly between the prongs. "Eight hundred thousand volts should do the trick."

Some people at a nearby table heard the crackle and looked over at us. I scowled at Cody.

"Put it away," I told him. He saw the look in my eye and slipped it back in his pocket. "Lesson number one with weapons, always keep them a secret, don't *ever* let anyone know what you have, and never ever pull one out in public unless you're going to use it."

Cody's face turned red. "Sorry."

"Two reasons," I said. "First and most important, if there's a bad guy scouting you out and he sees what type of protection you have, he can plan for it, figure out a way around it. And second, if a cop sees you and thinks you're a threat, you're gonna be the guy getting tasered, or he might just shoot you, or at the very least cuff you and dis-arm you, and get an explanation later. Either way you're out of business. So while we're on the subject Cody, do you have a gun?"

He shook his head. "No gun." He looked sullen, his face went slack, looked down at the table, and I waited for him to continue. "I'm a felon and on probation, I did something stupid when I was a kid so I can't get caught with a gun in my possession or I go straight to jail for five years."

I didn't ask what stupid thing he did, and he didn't offer it. It was none of my business. I was pretty damn stupid when I was a kid, and I was also pretty lucky to still be alive in spite of my stupidity.

I turned back to Tony. "What about Kalia, how does she fit with your team?"

"She's the inside person mostly, close to Gale, they get along well, and in a way are best friends. I'm on the outside, on the perimeter. I like it that way. Kind of like you from what I hear."

It was true, I did like to be out on the perimeter, identify and take out trouble long before it got anywhere near the client. In a lot of ways it was safer to be on the outside without anyone knowing who you were, but ever since I went solo I had to revise the way I operated.

"I've changed my job description. I provide a full service security package from the inside out with the boats as the vehicles of choice. People want to get out on the water and have some fun, maybe take a ride down to Mexico for the week, or cruise out here to Catalina, or some of the other west coast ports and visit some bars and restaurants without fear of someone jumping them from the shadows and robbing them on the dock. That's where I come in. Sort of the poor man's secret service detail. Plus I like being on the water. In a way, the ocean is like a perimeter if you know how to use it."

I put a twenty dollar bill under my glass and got up to leave. "I'll see you at the show."

Sliding my mirrored sunglasses over my nose, I watched the entire room and the mirror behind the bar through the corners of my eyes to see if anyone was paying unusual attention to my leaving. All seemed clear.

Time to go to work.

I decided to walk up the hill to the house rather than take a cab. It was only about half a mile to the Zane house, and of course it was uphill, but that made it all the better since I could walk slower without anyone thinking it was unusual, and take in more of the sights.

Walking lets you observe things you normally wouldn't pick up if you were driving or riding in a car. You can hear and smell and even feel your surroundings, and if you pay close attention to the peripheral view you may see something that can make the difference between living and dying.

I set my face as neutral and un-aggressive as I could while I walked. I didn't want someone to look at me and think, hey that guy's angry, stranger danger, etc. I was a happy guy. In fact I even whistled a little Christmas tune, tis the season to be jolly, while I strode up the hill and greeted with an easy smile anyone who crossed my path.

The road went straight up the hill past small, quaint homes that were squashed tight together with maybe ten feet of space between the rooflines. Most were newly painted, with little porches in the front, no grass lawns since water was scarce on the arid island, but mostly terra-scape with tough drought hardy plants and flowering cacti.

I took a turn onto Chimes Tower Road and headed up the slight incline that zigged and zagged.

The Zane house was set out on its own, on a steep rocky hill overlooking the harbor. There were no homes on either side or behind it but a road that wound around it led to the next cove over. There was a small garage below the home that looked like it had room to park about ten cars. Their plan was to shuttle everyone to the party from a central parking area set up in the center of the town.

I continued up the road as it wound around the hill until I was headed east. The east side of the home, faced the road, had a concrete stairway leading up to the pool deck where I assumed the party would be held. Two small catering trucks were parked next to the staircase and workers were hustling supplies up to the deck.

I walked all the way past the home until I couldn't see it anymore. Above me I could hear the caterers getting the party ready, tables and chairs being moved into place, sound systems being checked.

The hill was composed of light brown loose and rocky soil covered with scrub brush and cactus. Someone could scrabble up this way and enter the party, I made a note to keep an eye on this route when I was up on the deck. I walked a couple-hundred feet farther to a hairpin turn in the road, and the scenic overlook.

To the left was Descanso Bay and the beach club spread out in front of another crystal clear cove. Down the hill and over a steep cliff was the top of the adobe red round roof of the Avalon Casino and Theatre, and to the right was the harbor. I could see the Sugar riding safe and secure at her mooring along with all the other boats pointing east towards the on-shore winds.

Satisfied with my reconnaissance I headed back down and around the hill to the shuttle drop off.

The entrance to the party was roped off with red velvet ropes attached to gold stanchions, and two well-dressed young people were checking invitations and ID's. I showed them both of mine and they smiled and welcomed me inside. As far as they knew I was just another guest and that's the way it would be for the rest of the night. I was just another nameless, faceless guest and I would be on the perimeter, watching.

The place was all decked out with balloons and flowers. Pink and blue ribbons around every post, draped from the facia, and around a double sided baby stroller next to table number one; a not so subtle hint to the bride and groom what this was all about. Thirty round tables spread around the pool for the dinner guests, each with a number in the middle.

I looked at my ticket, it read twenty nine. About as far away from the action and attention as you could get, which was perfect, but it didn't matter since I wasn't planning on sitting. There was a stage for the band, portable wood parquet dance floor, with five foot squares that interlock together, with a bar on either side, and a long banquet table loaded with food.

It seemed cramped for three hundred people, why they didn't have the party in a bigger space was a mystery to me. But not enough of a mystery for me to spend another moment thinking about it.

With a quick eye I looked for danger spots, safe spots, places to hide, escape routes, places to hide weapons, things I could grab if I had to whack someone. I decided that if we had to get out of there and get out of there fast, we wouldn't take either of the two staircases leading to the road; those could be pincer spots, ambush points. Instead, we'd go up and over the hill to the scenic overlook and then down that hill to the casino. There was a narrow lanai in front of a bedroom on the ocean side of the home, and on the other side of the house a short wall that we could leap over. If we had to, we could climb on top of the cabana and get to the scrub hill by that route.

A waiter came by with a tray of champagne and I declined.

"Got anything stronger? I need something with a little bite to it."

"The bar is open sir if you'd like to get something else."

I did, and walked over to the one on the right. "Scotch and soda on ice, hold the scotch. Please," I added and winked at the pretty barmaid.

She was dressed in a starched white tuxedo shirt with a bow tie, nearly busting out at the seams at all the right places and she blushed as I looked at her.

A linen cloth covered an eight-foot table in front of her, lined up along its length were the usual intoxicants: a wide variety of whiskeys and rums, tequilas, vodkas, and gins.

Behind her was another table lined with red wine bottles, while the white wines and champagnes were stacked neatly in two giant ice chests, with another three giant ice chests packed with green beer bottles.

"Looks like you're ready for battle. Are

you?"

"I sure hope so."

"I heard the crowd's gonna be in the three hundred range." I pointed to the other bar where the bartender, a young man was getting his ice ready. "A hundred fifty per bar."

"I'm hoping that most of the people take the champagne that's being passed around. That should give us some breathing room if the going gets tough."

"At least you don't have any blended drinks." I looked behind the bar. "Do you?"

She brought her finger to her lips. "Shhhh. I have a blender under the bar but I'm hoping no-one asks for a blended."

I smiled at her. "It's our little secret." I made my way to the perimeter of the event and found a little nook out of the way where I would stay for the duration.

Soon the house and deck filled with well-dressed people of all ages, drinking and laughing and telling tall tales. The bartenders did their best to keep the drinks flowing and yet there was a constant line in front of the bar, until they rolled out the food, and then the crowd switched to the buffet.

I watched the perimeter with one eye and the party with the other as the sun set over the island in the west. It was actually a perfect place for an event like this, with the view over the harbor and the lights from all the boats on the water. On two different occasions I was approached by women looking for conversation, or something more, and each time I politely told them I was waiting for someone.

Gale's performance lasted nearly an hour, all throughout the meal, in fact, she was the entire dinner show. Her band consisted of a piano, an electric bass, a violin, and her golden voice.

She sang, she joked, she toasted the young newlyweds. She looked fantastic. She was wearing a skin tight silver cocktail dress that shimmered with her every movement and accentuated her abundant curves.

The dress was so tight that it looked like she'd either been poured into it, or had it painted right onto her skin. The martial arts training was having a very positive effect on her figure.

At the end of her last song the crowd of three hundred gave her a standing ovation, and she held the high note of the finale until she literally ran out of breath. Then it was time to cut the cake, fling the bouquet and the garter belt into the crowd, and fire up the rock and roll band for dancing into the night.

As the rock band was plugging in and tuning up, getting ready to play, I noticed one of the tables on the southern edge of the gala getting a little rowdy.

The banquet area was set up with thirty round tables for ten each, and this table had a group of fifteen young men bunched up on one side playing cards, and it looked like one of the guys was taking a beating while the rest of them were laughing at his expense.

He sat straight backed and high in his chair

and I could tell he was a sizeable man, his beefy large face was beet red and it didn't look like it was from a sunburn. It looked like they were playing poker, seven card stud with two cards down and four cards up. They were down to the last bet.

There were two men remaining for the hand they were playing and they sat facing each other with a small mountain of greenbacks in between them. I didn't see any ones, five's or ten dollar bills, they all looked larger, like twenties, fifties and hundreds.

The dealer laid a single card face down in front of each of the two players, who each took a quick look and made their last and final bets. When they turned the face-down cards up, the bystanders roared and by the look of beet faced player's face, the devil took him over. He jumped to his feet, pushed back his chair, reached around to grab the back of it, and with a swift motion lifted it high over his head. He swung it around and slammed it straight down on the table, breaking the chair in splinters and sending the cards and money flying in the air.

Someone shouted, "No Corbin!" Then he reached across the table, grabbed at his opponents neck and punched him in the face with a solid right cross. You could hear the crack of the fist against cheek bone clear across the room.

The poor guy was overmatched and went straight over backwards onto the ground, still sitting in his chair. Corbin leapt around the table, pouncing on top of the guy's chest and landed a few more straight punches until a wall of men pulled him off and held him back, two men on each arm and two on his neck. He was frothing at the mouth and speaking in tongues like a beast released from a cage. It was everything the six men could do to hold him back.

The band stopped warming up and the people in the crowd stood on their feet, craning over each other to see what the commotion was all about on the edge of the party. Some of the men hustled Corbin out of the area and towards the stairway leading down to the entrance and the small parking lot. The others in their group put the chairs back in place and helped the beaten man to his feet and sat him back in his chair.

He had a reddish purple swollen cheek and blood at the corner of his mouth. He pushed his helpers away and held a napkin to his face, humiliated.

The father of the bride climbed up on stage in front of the microphone and tapped on it with his finger to see if it was live. He was a short burly man with a handlebar moustache and a large glass full of beer in his right hand.

"Alright everyone, looks like Corbin had a little too much jungle juice."

The crowd laughed uneasily at the little joke, and the father raised his glass in a toast. "Let's give another round of applause for the bride and groom and get ready for the first dance."

The crowd applauded mightily and whooped and whistled. They turned their attention to watch as the bride and groom made their way to the dance floor, the crowd parting like the Egyptian Red Sea.

I decided to follow Corbin and his handlers out to the parking lot to make sure he actually left the premises. I wanted to make sure he didn't decide to grab a gun and come back to shoot the place up, and potentially have a stray bullet hit one of us, or Gale, who was talking with a group of people near the stage. When someone gets that heated up you have to make absolutely certain they weren't going to cause any more trouble.

Unless it was a well-planned diversion, I thought. Anything was possible.

Trying to get the protection to move away from the protected. I considered that scenario for a moment and then put it aside. The guy that got punched in the face looked thoroughly shaken, and you couldn't fake the rage in Corbin's face while he was attacking the guy.

Not to me anyways.

I took a quick inventory of the pummeled guy, his condition both physical and mental. He might also be one to have a gun and decide to pull it out and start firing away in heated revenge after getting beaten and humiliated. It wouldn't be the first time something like that happened, but he looked harmless and utterly defeated, and so I kept walking.

I moved through the tables and along the tree line to get a view of the makeshift parking lot on the street. Somehow they'd managed to fit quite a few vehicles into a small space.

There were dozens of cars lined up neatly, mixed in with twice as many golf carts, which was the preferred method, and for many the only form of transportation available on the island.

Two men were talking with Corbin as he leaned his back against a small shiny black truck with a bright yellow paddle board strapped to the racks on top. He had his arms folded across his chest and was nodding as one of the men talked to him. It was the man who gave a toast earlier in the evening, a sergeant with the Avalon police department.

From their body language the deputy was giving 'ol Corbin a steady and thorough dressing down. Corbin however didn't look too worried, his face was stoic, with a red and shiny alcohol flush. He alternated nodding and shaking his head as his preferred method of communication. His lips did not move. After one last nod of his head and a shrug of his shoulders, he opened the driver's side door of the truck, started the engine, backed out of his space, and drove slowly down the hill.

I took three things from seeing this.

First, Corbin was a hothead, and he was also big and strong as an ox, which made for a dangerous combination if you ever got on the wrong side of him as we all just witnessed.

Second, he had a car on Catalina so he must have lived on the island for a long time. There are less than six hundred cars allowed on the island. To get one, you have to put your name on a list, and the wait time for a permit is somewhere around fifteen years. Someone has to die or move away for you to move up the list.

Third, a police sergeant just let a guy who'd been drinking, was obviously drunk, and who had brutally assaulted someone with a chair and his fists, just climb right in that car of his and drive away.

Corbin was connected.

I went back to the party to check on Gale. She was saying her goodbyes to the wedding party, kissing each of them on the cheek, and waving to everyone else as she moved gracefully towards the exit. She'd planned it this way: she would sing and entertain for an hour and when the dance band was ready to play she would leave the party.

"It's better that way," she said. "Otherwise I'll get in the way, and I'm not supposed to be the center of attention, the bride and groom are."

We bundled into two taxis at the entrance and headed down the hill to the hotel where Gale could change into comfortable travelling clothes, and then off to the heliport.

The chartered helicopter was a twin engine S-76 Sikorsky, the interior was all lit up. The pilot and co-pilot were in the cockpit looking at their clip-boards and going through their pre-flight routine.

Tony and Kali got on board, sitting in the two back seats, followed by Rhonda and Garrett.

The four of us lingered at the stairs. Gale reached out and hugged Amber, and I shook

Cody's hand.

It was more of a military de-briefing than a goodbye as I turned to Gale. "So, you look good. I talked to Tony about your self-defense training and it sounds like you're doing the right things. Just remember, the best self-defense in the world is staying alert, keeping your eyes open, and steering clear of danger well before it gets anywhere close to you." I nodded at Cody. "Keep your feet firm on the deck and your eyes on the bow, right?"

"You got that right captain."

Gale's face turned serious. "You know Badger, last year when I was kidnapped and strapped into the chair on the second floor of that filthy tattoo shop with a gun pointed at my head, the world was very small at that moment. It's like every bit of time and space in the entire universe, everything that had ever been and ever would be was squeezed into the space the size of the little black hole at the end of the barrel of that gun. I was going to die right then and there. I expected a bullet to fire out of it any moment, and it's like time was standing still in a long and horrible everlasting moment. And then I saw you come through the door, in the corner of my eyes I could see you, and it was like an angel was sent from heaven to save me."

Tears filled her eyes at the memory and she reached out and grabbed me, hugged me tight, and lightly sobbed.

Amber and Cody looked on uneasily, and then she wiped her eyes with the sleeve of her shirt and patted me on the shoulder.

"I love you for that." Then the moment passed and she laughed nervously as she noticed everyone looking at her. "I'm sorry everyone, I just got a little emotional." She clarified her statement, pointing at Cody. "I'm in love with you mister, and I know that Amber is in love with you, Badger and you're in love with her, but I do love you for saving me, and I always will." She threw her hair back in defiance. "And I'm not ashamed to say it."

Amber reached out and gave her a hug.

"This always happens after weddings," said Cody. "The girls get all sensitive."

Gale playfully punched him on the arm.

"Actually," she said. "It's not really a love type of feeling, it's something more and I can't really explain it or put it in the right kind of words. It's something beyond love if that makes sense. I tell you it's almost religious."

"The way I look at it," I said. "We got lucky pure and simple, getting out of there alive. Call it divine providence or whatever you want, we lucked out, we know it, and that's the basis of being humble."

Gale hugged me one more time and headed up the stairs. "We'll see you again soon," she said.

"Stay safe." I pointed at Cody as they climbed the steps into the helicopter, he nodded and pointed back to me, his face somber.

Since I was in the protection business, I studied theories about protectors and the protected and victims and rescuers until I was cross-eyed, and from what I'd digested from volumes of work on the subject, it was impossible to put a label on any one situation. But they all had a common thread and one thing was certain, we were connected for the rest of time, like siblings, or parents and their children. We were family.

Amber and I walked back to the taxi as the helicopter's engines revved and it lifted into the air, washing us with a gust of wind and dust, then turned its nose to the East, and flew off into the black sky.

2.

We spent the night on the boat and woke to the sound of flocks of seagulls crying out to the sunrise as they flew overhead, searching for food.

We stretched, made coffee and breakfast, and sat on the deck to watch the morning glow in the east and the last of the stars fade away over the island in the west.

It looked like it was going to be a nice day.

Amber didn't have be back to work at the hospital until tomorrow night so we decided to take a slow and leisurely sail around the island before heading back to Dana Point early the next morning.

We left Avalon harbor at seven in the morning with the sun rising over the ocean to the east. We went northwest along the coast with a fifteen knot west wind on our port side.

The island of Catalina is twenty-two miles long and eight miles wide at its widest point. I figured the fifty-mile sail would take around eight hours and we could spend the night back at Avalon before heading back across the channel to the California time zone the next morning.

Everything was slower here on the island and I kind of liked the pace. I didn't want to leave too soon.

At nine-thirty in the morning we passed about half a mile outside of Two Harbors. Here, the island pinched together until it was only about seven hundred and fifty yards across with a small harbor on each side. We passed the eastern side of the harbor, which held around twenty five boats of various sizes. It looked like there were enough empty mooring buoys for another fifteen vessels. I made a mental note to bring the Sugar here for a night or two sometime in the near future.

At ten-thirty we rounded the tip of Arrow point, tacked into the wind and then headed along the north side of the island just outside the jumbled rocks of Strawberry Cove.

At eleven we found the body floating in the ocean.

You see a lot of things floating in the water these days. Trash from ships, trash from shore, plastic bottles and cans. Chairs, pallets, baggies, nets, you name it. But you don't usually see a body floating.

I saw the object far off on our starboard side, every now and then bobbing to the top of the crest of a wave and then disappearing into the trough.

It was orange, and bright, and bigger than most things you see on the water so I pinched into the wind to get closer to it and have a look. When it went by the starboard hull we could see it was a woman in a life vest.

It had to be a woman. She was wearing a white wetsuit, had long dark black hair, and was face down in the water. Lifeless.

"Oh my God," Amber muttered and brought her hand to her mouth.

I pulled the boat straight into the wind, hit the winches, lowered the sails, started the engine, and motored back to where she was floating. I toggled the forward and back thruster until we were right alongside her, then tried to figure out how to get her on board.

Now, getting someone who is alive, willing and able to help you get them up and over the gunwale and onto a yacht that's sitting high off the water line is one thing. Getting a body that is heavy and filled with water is another thing altogether.

She was dead, there was no doubt whatsoever about that. I could call the Coast Guard and wait for them to get a boat out here to do the recovery, but I wanted to get the body out of the water before a shark came around. I quickly scanned the horizon, there was not a single other boat in sight as far as I could see.

"Where in the heck did she come from?" I wondered out loud. I worried that her boat probably sank, and there more bodies out there floating around.

Every boat on the water has a deck hook on board to grab things that are out of reach, like mooring balls and ropes and docks, and other boats to bring them close. It's a long extendable pole with a non-sharp big and round hook on the end. I unlashed it from the side of the deck, reached down and hooked her right under the shoulder pad of the life vest. Some good it had done her.

She might have weighed around ninety to a hundred pounds on dry land, but out here, with her lungs and belly filled with heavy sea water she weighed close to two hundred.

I braced my feet on the swaying deck, gently lifted her out of the water, and slid her backside onto the deck of the boat.

Now Amber, a nurse, sees a lot of gruesome things in the hospital: gunshot wounds, stabbings, burn cases, broken bones, but even she was shocked and turned her face away for a moment before she could look again.

Water streamed out of the woman's mouth and nose. The skin on her face was thick and pasty white with grey splotches, puffy and swollen from being in the water for who knows how long. At least a day, maybe longer.

There were little bite marks all over her exposed face and neck and hands, from some sort of sea creatures, small fish or eels feeding on her corpse as it floated on the surface. Chunks of white flesh hanging by threads.

"She looks Chinese," I said. "Hard to say how old she was but I'm guessing she was probably in her late twenties." It was terrible to see. "We'll call the Coast Guard and get under way back to Avalon. I'll cover her with a blanket, lash her to the deck, and we'll motor back."

Amber made a funny sound and ran to the back of the boat. She threw up over the side.

I went down to the cabin, and got a couple of blankets and some bungee cords from the storage, and got back on deck.

I did some quick calculations and decided to wrap her in the blankets to keep her intact and then secure her with as many bungees as it took.

As I was tucking the first blanket under her I noticed the corner of a large zip locked baggie sticking out from under the life vest. It was wedged in pretty well so I pulled gently at the corner until it came out, and laid it on her chest.

There were only three items in the bag and I opened it to get a closer look. There was a California driver's license, a blue Social Security card, and a two inch thick stack of money. Tens, twenties and hundreds, mostly hundreds though, and as I flipped through the stack I figured there must be around eight or ten thousand dollars all wrapped in a thick rubber band.

I looked carefully at the driver's license. It said Mei Young Lee, 2575 Bay Shore Avenue, Long Beach, California.

Talk about a small world. I know the street. It's in Belmont Shores, a tightly packed oceanside community next to the Alamitos Bay Marina in Long Beach. The street is right next to the water on the marina. I've parked the Spice there at the harbor, and walked along that very street to the beach.

To the west and a couple of hundred yards off the beach sit four man-made islands where they still pump oil from a reserve under the ocean. You can see the Queen Mary permanently berthed across the bay on the south side of the Port of Los Angeles, one of the busiest ports in the world, where all the container ships from Asia unload their cargo. I have a friend who works on the docks unloading the ships, seven days a week, day after grinding day.

She was a local girl. An Angelino.

"So what are you doing in the water with ten thousand cash in a bag?" I asked Mei Young Lee, but she did not respond. I resealed and gently stuffed the bag back under the life vest where I found it, and covered her with the blanket.

Amber came forward and helped me bungee tie the body to the deck and then went back to the shade of the wheel house and hid her face in her hands.

"You never get used to it," she said as I joined her, fired up the engine, and set a course back around the top of the island.

"What's that?"

"Seeing someone in that condition."

"But you're a nurse."

"My patients normally continue to live, and leave the hospital still breathing. But every once in a while..." And her voice trailed off. "I'm telling you straight, that you never get used to it." And she stared off into the horizon.

I turned the radio frequency to the Coast Guard channel sixteen. "Mayday, mayday, mayday," I repeated in succession, and when I got a response from their dispatch, I gave our vessel's name, our position and the nature of the emergency, although it wasn't really an emergency any more. For Mei Young Lee, that time had passed.

When we rounded the north corner of the island we could see the Coast Guard cutter barreling full speed towards us, quickly closing the gap within a few minutes. When they were just about on top of us, I idled our boat and they circled around and pulled up alongside to assess the situation.

I can see now how they closed the gap so fast. Their boat is one of the new response boats, all lightweight aluminum construction, forty-five feet in length, twin diesel engines with waterjet propulsion and able to get up to forty-three knots, which is nearly fifty miles per hour on the water.

They have to be able to outrun the drug smugglers, or at least keep pace with them.

Machine gun turret mounts on the front and back of the boat, able to roll over completely and self-right. The kind of boat I'd like to have someday.

Soft fenders run the full length of their boat so they can come alongside another boat on the high seas, without damaging the hull, and quickly board that vessel. Two crewmen reached out with tender hooks and brought our boats together.

"Permission to come aboard sir," a sharply dressed officer asked and I waved him on. He was carrying a clipboard and a waterproof bag the size of an attaché case.

Lieutenant Myles Johnson read his name tag. We shook hands and I brought him forward to the bungeed blankets. He pulled the cover down and looked for a moment at her face before covering her again. He let out a sigh while shaking his head.

I guess he never got used to the sight either.

I pointed to her life vest. "She has an ID in a bag with a big wad of money stuffed right under here. It was poking out when I pulled her in, so I took a look."

I realized then that it was evidence and I shouldn't have touched it with my bare fingers.

He used a pen from his pocket to lift the edge of the vest. When he confirmed the bag was there, he pulled out a pair of latex gloves from his front pocket, slid them on, and pulled out the bag. He opened it and looked at the driver's license, the blue Social Security card, and the stack of money, then re-sealed it and put it in the waterproof bag that he carried on-board.

"I'm not a doctor," he said in a low voice, "but I'm guessing she's been in the water for a couple of days."

"That's what I was thinking. I didn't want to risk waiting for you guys to get here, so I brought her on board."

"You did the right thing. Thank you."

Rather than try to transfer the body at sea,

we decided it would be best if we both docked at Two Harbors and from there they would take charge of the deceased.

Lt. Johnson would ride with us and interview us at the same time.

Introductions were made and hands shaken again.

"Lieutenant Myles Johnson, ma'am, sir."

"Amber Clark."

"Badger Thompson."

He eyed me closer, and repeated it. "Badger, you mean like the animal?"

I nodded, "It's a long story."

I started up the engine and we got under way, heading east in the lee of the island towards Two Harbors, with the cutter leading the way five boat lengths in front of us.

He sat down on the leeward side of the nook and started writing. "Sorry, this is a formality. I'll need your full names, addresses, phone numbers, ship registration, nautical position where the body was found, sea conditions, and any other details you can think of that might help us in our investigation."

He went through the list and we answered everything to the best of our knowledge, and when he was satisfied that he'd gleaned all the info he could get out of us, we were nearly at Two Harbors.

"What happens next?" I asked him.

"We'll transport the body back to Avalon and turn it over to the police department. This is their jurisdiction, we are only assisting in this recovery operation. The body will be taken to the mortuary and they'll put it on ice until the next of kin can be notified. They'll probably have an autopsy due to the circumstances. They have procedures set in place since people die over here all the time. Mostly from old age, rarely from drowning. The mortuary can assist with cremation, burial, or transport the body back to the mainland for burial there. It's up to the family."

"Anyone been reported missing at sea lately? Any boats missing?"

He shook his head. "None that we're aware of. It's been a pretty slow couple of days actually. This is our first search and rescue or recovery in three days. We were actually getting ready to do a drill just to keep the crew sharp when we got your call."

"Strange that she would be out here with no one reporting her missing," said Amber

"Yes, that is strange," he said.

He hesitated for a minute, looking at Amber, seemingly deciding whether he should continue.

"But it's not the first time we've seen this. About two years ago an old retired couple cruising on their boat out of Long Beach found a body in the same general location. An oriental man in his mid-thirties, wearing a wetsuit and a life vest. No one reported him missing and they never found out who he was. Maybe we'll get lucky with this woman and find out what she was doing out there from her next of kin."

"I sure would like to know," I said. "If only

because I'm the one who found her. I feel responsible in a way, and I can't have question marks hanging over my head. Makes it hard to sleep at night."

I followed the Coast Guard ship into the harbor and parked right behind it on the long wooden jetty. They put her in a black plastic body bag, with blankets and all, zipped it up, carried her on board, and stowed her in a cabinet at the back.

There was a stain where she'd been lying on the deck and two of the Coast Guard sailors jumped on board and scrubbed it clean with scrub brushes and a hose from the dock. Soon there was no sign that she'd ever been there.

"Well it looks like you're ship shape and ready to go. Thanks for all your help in this recovery. We'd better get back to Avalon right away," said the Lt. and shook each of our hands again. "We'll be in contact if we need additional information, and I'll let you know if we find out anything about what she was doing out there, with the family's permission of course."

"Thanks, I'd appreciate that," I said.

He handed me his business card with the official seal of the Coast Guard and his cell phone and e-mail address. "You can contact me anytime. I'm attached to this post for the next six months. Hopefully we'll have closure within that time frame."

We watched their boat pull out of the harbor, slowly at first. When it was past the break wall it went into high gear and roared off down the coast to Avalon.

The curious crowd that had gathered around the pier to watch had filtered away, leaving us alone.

"What do you want to do now?" I asked Amber. "Do you want to stay here for the night, it's a pretty nice little harbor, or sail back to Avalon?"

She seemed in a daze, her eyes were glazed over as she watched the Coast Guard boat disappear out of sight, and then sighed heavily before replying. "I definitely do not want to spend the night in Avalon, not tonight anyways. Not with that body in the morgue on the hill. Kind of freaks me out to be honest. I think I just want to go home. I'm afraid I'm going to have a nightmare over this, and if so I'd rather be in my own house tonight."

I wanted to poke her in the ribs, ruffle up her hair, and loosen her up a bit. Lighten her mood, but thought better of it and got the boat ready for the open sea. I coiled the ropes, started the engine, and motored out of the harbor. I set the sails outside the break wall.

It was a quiet journey home. We sailed on a broad reach all the way over to Dana Point on a northwest wind, riding downwind, down swell all the way like a blue and white wind wave highway. The steady rocking of the hull became mesmerizing. Amber went forward into the berth, fell asleep an hour into the journey, and didn't wake up until I winched down the sails and started the engine to pull into the harbor as the sun set on the horizon.

We drove up the hill to our little house. As I tucked her into bed she pulled the covers far over her head to hide from the night.

3.

2575 Bayshore Avenue in Long Beach. The address stuck in my mind as I sat at the table having breakfast with Amber, and I could see clearly in my mind's eye the driver's license with the picture of the local Chinese girl from L.A. It was the last thing I thought about before I went to sleep last night and the first thing I thought about when I woke up this morning. I couldn't shake it out of my mind.

It was only yesterday that we'd found her in the water, and yet it seemed like a year ago. In some ways it didn't even seem real.

"How'd you sleep?" I asked Amber as I took a sip of coffee and watched her carefully over the edge of the cup. I wanted to be gentle with her since she'd gotten so shaken up over the incident.

She held out her hand and wobbled it. "So-so I guess. I did a lot of tossing and turning and I don't even know if I actually slept or not to tell you truth. I don't remember having any bad dreams so that's a good thing. How about you, did you sleep okay?"

I wobbled my hand also. "I slept great except for the tossing and turning, you wacked me in the face a couple of times but I survived."

She brought her hand to her mouth. "I'm so sorry!"

"Just kidding, sugar. Your tossing and turning is like a butterfly fluttering it's wings on a rainbow covered cloud, how's that?"

She kissed me on the top of my head and took away the plates. "I'm heading to work early today and it's a good thing that we came back yesterday after all. One of the other nurses called in sick so I can pick up some extra hours. What are you planning today?"

I was staring blankly out the window and still thinking about the dead girl's driver's license.

"I'm not sure yet," I said, still staring out the window.

But I was sure. I was heading up the coast to Belmont Shores. I just didn't want to tell Amber where I was going. I didn't want to stir things up, and bring up bad memories. She seemed to be in good spirits and looking forward to work, and since she wanted to forget about finding Mei Young Lee, I kept my plans quiet. Some things are better left unsaid.

"You could always come to the hospital and see where I work, look at the newborn babies in the maternity ward. "

"Me, in a hospital? Not a chance. I wouldn't go near a hospital if my life depended on it. Sure, I like the people that work in hospitals, the doctors, nurses, especially you. I just don't like the inside of the buildings, the lights, the walls, the quiet, it creeps me out, too antiseptic. Even walking down a hallway seems like a morgue."

"You make it sound terrible."

"Do you like your new hospital?"

"It's okay, the people are nice, but the building is kind of old. The elevators need repair and stick mid-floor sometimes."

"See? Hospitals are dangerous."

She brought the coffee pot, filled my cup, and patted me on the head. "Poor little scaredy-cat."

When I looked back over to the kitchen, she was rinsing the dishes in the sink. Tawny silk brown hair pulled tight in a French bun, her nursing uniform taught and snug on the edges, inviting curves.

I smiled at my good fortune.

"You know, you're looking pretty good in that nursing uniform right about now. Maybe you should go to work a little later and we can lounge around the house for a while. Talk about things."

"Nice try sailor. I'll have to take a rain check on that. Try me again in two days?"

I shook my head in dismay. Timing was everything, and this time I was out of luck.

"Well, in that case I think I'll take a ride on the chopper. Get some fresh air, then come back and work on one of the boats."

I'd been on the water for the past two days and it was always good to mix it up a bit and put some rubber on the road.

And there was a house I needed to see.

2575 Bayshore Avenue: why were you in the water with ten thousand in cash?

I kissed Amber goodbye, put on my boots and leather jacket and went downstairs to the garage. I fired up the chopper and revved the engine a couple of times. It sounded great. The seismic pop of the pistons pulsing on my skin and shaking my bones down to my boots. Deep throated, loud, and mean everyone would hear me coming from a long way away.

Some people hated the sound of a chopper.

I loved it, and revved the engine one more time before pulling the clutch and putting it in gear.

Pacific Coast Highway winds along the coast through small and big towns all the way from the border of San Diego to the top of the state. It's a blast to ride a motorcycle on it, especially a double banger.

I revved the engine by the basketball courts in Laguna Beach and got some worried looks from blue haired old ladies and grins from the local beach bums. I blasted the sound barrier in Huntington Beach in front of the pier, and before I knew it I was in Long Beach pulling into Belmont Shores, pride of the coast.

I parked the bike on the opposite side of the street from 2575 and stretched my legs and neck, reached out and cracked my knuckles. It had taken an hour to travel twenty-five miles and I felt great.

There was an on-shore west wind blowing

from the ocean just two hundred yards away and the air was fragrant with the heavy smell of salt water, sun tan lotion, and asphalt. The beaches were packed with day trippers, surfers and bikinis, while the newly paved roadways melted under the hot California sun.

The houses were small, every shape and color, and scrunched tight together. But nearly all of them are in perfect condition: newly painted, windows sparkling. This is a bedroom community on the edge of Los Angeles, highly sought after due to its beachside location, and very pricey.

I don't know what I expected to find. A black wreath on the door. Mourning relatives streaming into the house wearing black. A flag at half-mast.

The neighbor across the street was in his garage checking me out with one eye, while polishing the fender of a large silver truck. It looked like a four car garage and was bigger than most others on the block, with a red Ferrari, a couple of dirt bikes and three jet skis. He also had a street bike parked in the back of the garage, the chrome gleaming even in the shade. I wondered if he ever rode it. There must have been some serious cash in his back pocket with all the expensive toys.

The guy was a real sports vehicle junkie. He was gazing out from the cool shadows, trying to determine if I'm a friend or foe, dressed as I am, in a leather jacket on a chopper.

I gave him a polite wave, and he waved back and then put down his towel, wiped his hands on his pants and started across the street.

He was a tough looking guy, big and muscle bound, short cropped hair, walking with a swagger that told me he's trained in some sort of martial arts. A lot of people are these days, but this is one son of a bitch I wouldn't want to meet in a dark alley. He sees my eyes and smiles to show that he means no trouble.

"Nice bike," he says. "Is that an Eighty-Eight?"

I nod my head, he got the engine size right, eighty-eight cubic inches of firepower. "Yep, Twin Cam eighty-eight. Kind of old, but still kicking it down the road."

"That engine's bad ass," he said. "I had one for a lot of years and just traded up to the new Twin Cam ninety-six. They're both excellent motors."

"You ride?"

"Every chance I get. Once a year we get a bunch of guys together and do a thousand-mile loop, up to the Oregon border, through all the woods and back roads."

"Nice neighborhood here, I'll bet some of these house are worth about what, a million bucks?"

"Try two million and change for the cheapest one," he said. "But the taxes will kill you. Are you looking for a place to buy, thinking about moving into the neighborhood?"

I could tell he was trying to find out what I was doing here without really asking so I saved him the trouble and got right to the point.

"A friend of mine lives in that house," and I

pointed to the house three doors down from his. "Chinese girl, Mei Young Lee."

His face scrunched up, puzzled. "How long ago?"

"I don't know, like yesterday."

"That house?" He pointed directly at it. "You sure you got the right address?"

"Pretty sure, 2575 Bayshore Avenue."

"There's no Chinese girl at that house."

The hackles on the back of my neck stood up and I tried to stay calm and not show my inner alarm with my body language. Something was wrong here, I could feel it. My guard went up.

"I don't know," I said. "It's been a couple of years since I saw her, maybe she moved, but that was the address she gave me, I'm sure of it."

He shook his head. "Look buddy, I've lived here twenty five years and there's never been a Chinese girl living at that house as long as I've been here. The Andersons live there now, they bought the place ten years ago, check it out, here come some of their kids."

And right on cue two blond toe-headed pre-teen boys raced up the street from the beach barefooted, hand-fighting to get to the porch first, and careened through the screen door of the house and slammed it behind them, yelling for their Mom to make them some food.

"Before that it was the Calvin's, and they definitely weren't Chinese either."

He was looking sideways at me now, sizing me up.

I shrugged my shoulders. "I've never

actually been here. She just gave me the address and said to stop by if I was ever in town. Maybe I got the wrong address, my mistake."

"Maybe you got the wrong street."

"This is Bayshore Avenue right?"

"Yes, but there's a Bay*view* Avenue a couple of blocks over. People always get them mixed up. Bayview, Bayshore, they sound pretty much the same."

Not a chance I thought. It was Bayshore on the license, no doubt about it, I don't make mistakes like that and I know what I saw, but I didn't want to argue with this guy. I found out what I needed to know.

I nodded my head in agreement, deep in thought, and then slapped the side of my skull with my hand. "I'm an idiot. You know you're right. It was Bayview, not Bayshore." I laughed at my mistake. "Maybe riding the bike up here rattled something loose up here." I grinned and pointed to my head. "Anyway it was nice to talk bikes with you."

He laughed along with me. "You know what they say, when you get older and start getting screws loose, it's time to start carrying a wrench."

I pointed at him and said, "You know I think you're right."

He held out his hand. "I'm Jack Wilson."

"Joe Smith," I lied. "I live in San Diego." Normally I would come up with a better alias than that, but it was the best I could come up with on short notice, I was still a bit startled at finding out that Mei Young Lee never lived here, or so this guy said. I was a natural born skeptic and decided I'd better look into this from another angle.

"Well, I better go a couple of blocks over and see if I can find her house. It's not a big deal if I don't, I'm just here on a whim. Thanks for your help."

I got on the bike and pushed the starter button and revved the engine a few times, gave him a crisp military salute and headed down the street towards the ocean.

More questions than answers.

Why were you in the water with ten thousand in cash *and* a fake I.D. Mei Young Lee?

Maybe I was sticking my nose where it didn't belong and I should forget about the whole thing and just walk away. Walk away and get back to protecting people that were still alive. Just walk away, Badger, I told myself for the third time, but I knew I was talking to a brick wall. I didn't walk away from things like this. It was a character flaw.

I hoped I didn't live to regret this, but had to get to the bottom of it.

I figured that maybe in a way I was protecting a dead girl.

At the corner of Bayshore and Pacific Coast Highway I took a left turn and headed south for a couple of hundred yards, pulled into an open parking space in front a large moving van, walked to the back of it, and looked around the corner. I got out my scope and aimed it at the guy's garage.

He was talking on the phone and gesturing with his free hand as he barked into the mouthpiece. He was calm and laughing when he was talking with me, but now he looked agitated, and angry. He looked towards the direction I'd taken with the chopper, but I was sure he couldn't see me.

The hackles on the back of my neck stood on end again.

4.

Eleven o'clock on a Sunday morning in the middle of summer is usually a nice, quiet time in the city of Avalon. Most of the weekend crowd had left early in the morning for the trip back home, and the rest would be gone before mid-afternoon. Locals would have a week of normal life with the island population at a manageable five thousand. By Friday afternoon though, things would change dramatically.

Next week was a four day holiday weekend.

The mainland ferries, private boats, and planes would deliver to its placid shores revelers in droves. Thousands of weekend vacationers, drinkers, and partiers came, and the streets would fill to capacity like Mardi Gras. The clubs and bars would be a place of music and laughing and singing through the night, along with the occasional fight here and there in relation to, and equivalent to, the amount of booze poured. The population of Avalon would swell from five thousand to fifteen to twenty thousand in the matter of hours on Friday afternoon into the night.

Deputy Police Chief Don Baker sat at his desk in his paneled, air-conditioned office, sorted through paperwork, and settled his mind before the onslaught. The Station Commander was on the mainland at a seminar in San Diego for a week, learning how to be a better Commander, leaving Don in charge.

Either way, it didn't really matter to Don since he was basically in charge all the time anyways. Being the Station Commander on Avalon was, in a way, a cherry pie position, a political appointment. Most of the guys who were assigned to the job had been on the force for a long time and were on their way out the door to retirement. This was the last stop.

Don stopped thinking about the Commander and got back to work. Thousands of people were heading to the island for the upcoming holiday weekend. He double-checked the schedule to make sure he had the manpower necessary to keep the peace in case it turned into a war zone.

Two Harbors would be a problem since it was so far away. There was only one officer on duty until Saturday night and if he had to respond to a fight at one of the bars or moored boats, and needed help, it took an hour to drive the twenty miles on the winding road with backup.

He double-checked the schedule again. Lenny was their guy on duty throughout the weekend and he was pretty much on top of it.

Lenny was a tough guy and he could handle himself in a fight, but he was also smart, and that was a key to being a good cop when you were on your own. You had to be smart and fast on your feet and find ways to head off problems before they became one in the first place.

The phone rang and he looked at the screen for the caller ID. It said 'Null' so the person on the other side had it blocked. He picked it up.

"Deputy Baker."

"We have a problem."

"What are you talking about?"

"Someone came looking for the Chinese girl. Said he knew her, she was an old friend, and that she gave him the address and told him to look her up sometime. Came riding up in a chopper, a real tough looking guy, square jaw, broken nose, looks ex-military, pretty sure he's packing a gun. Said he lives in San Diego."

"Son of a bitch," said Don.

"Yeah. Now you know why we put my neighbor's address on the ID's. If there's ever a problem I'm going to find out about it before it gets out of control. Not knowing is worse than knowing, right?"

"Who is this guy? Did you get his name?"

"Said his name was Joe Smith, can you believe it? A real lame attempt at an alias if I ever heard one. I know the bastard's lying. I got the license plate off the chopper though."

"Let me have it," said Don and he pulled up the California vehicle license database on his computer screen.

"17V8541," said the voice on the other end and the chief punched it in.

It took two seconds for the search to pull it up and there it was on the screen in black and white.

"Badger Thompson," said Don. "And the guy's address is a boat slip in the Dana Point Harbor. Slip number 345. Hold on." He pulled up another website, the state harbor database, punched in a code to gain access then scrolled down a list and clicked onto the Dana Point Harbor link. He scrolled down towards the bottom, and there it was, slip 345, registered to a Badger Thompson, for a forty-five foot sailboat named the 'Sugar'. And then it all clicked, he'd forgotten about the recovery report.

"He's the guy," said Don.

"What do you mean 'he's the guy'?," asked the agitated voice on the other end.

"I thought I recognized the name, he was on the Coast Guard recovery report. He's the boater who found the girl in the water yesterday. The captain of the Sugar. They're the ones who brought her into Two Harbors and transferred her to the Coast Guard ship. He must have searched her body and found the package she was carrying with the driver's license."

"I don't like this one bit."

"What do you want me to do?" asked Don.

"Nothing," said the voice. "You take care of Catalina, I'll take care of the mainland. Just keep things running smooth over there."

"When's our next shipment?"

"I'm not sure. Maybe next week, maybe the week after that. I'll let you know when they tell me."

"Look Jack, I know we've talked about this before. I'm thinking this might be my last run to the lane, this is getting a little too hairy."

There was silence on the other side for a moment and Don wondered if they were still connected.

"Are you still there?"

"I'm still here. Look, we'll talk about that when the time comes. For now just plan on being ready, and don't let us down. We'll figure something out. I'll be over there tonight with our payment for the last shipment. We'll meet at the club, as usual."

The phone on the other end clicked and Don sat there looking out the window. After a while he remembered to breathe again.

They were walking on a tightrope with this smuggling business. There were a lot of eyes on Catalina: the Coast Guard, FBI, and Homeland Security. Avalon was a jewel in the eyes of the state and no-one wanted anything to smudge it with dirt.

Five years without a hiccup until now.

Everything is running smooth until it isn't, and in a business like this, one little glitch could get you killed or thrown in jail for a long time. And in his case it'd be better to be dead, he knew what happened to cops in prison.

He had enough money in the bank to last for a long time if they were careful and didn't go on a hog wild spending spree, and with his side business, the bar in town, he was starting to make a little bit of cash on the side. He didn't need this smuggling business.

But he did need money, and a lot of it. For his wife Amanda. Or she might get bored and move on to greener pastures. She seemed moody and a little bit aloof to his romantic advances lately. A couple of weeks ago he sat her down and tried to reason with her, tried to get her to reign in her outrageous spending habits. Now he was getting the cold fish treatment in return.

He felt a dull pain in the middle of his stomach. He reached into the desk and pulled out a large plastic bottle and popped a large white tablet onto his tongue to calm down the burning sensation of the acid indigestion eating him alive from the inside out. All he needed was more pressure added to his already full plate.

"What the hell have I gotten myself into," he muttered.

5.

I rode over to the L.A. County Office of the Assessor on East Willow Street by the 405 freeway.

The clerk at the window was helpful. For two bucks a shot I could get a printout of the public data owner records for any property in the county. I had two in mind. 2575 Bayshore, and the neighbor that came out to talk to me, 2579 Bayshore.

You can find out anything about any property in the city. Who owns it, their mailing address, what they paid for it, what the assessed value is, the property taxes, any liens or mortgages on it, square footage, usage permitted. The only thing the public data sheet doesn't show is who actually resides in the home.

Sure enough the printout for 2575 showed that it was owned by Philip Anderson and his wife Kate. They bought it ten years ago, so the guy was telling the truth as far as that went anyways.

His house though, was owned by a corporation. Cobblestone Enterprises, LLC, with a PO Box in Long Beach for mail delivery.

I thanked the clerk, folded the papers into my back pocket and took off on the bike again. When I got back home and had access to a computer I'd look up Cobblestone Enterprises find out who owned it, who was a partner, employees, the works, and look at the Andersons, who were they, occupations, family ties, police and medical records. I could find out anything about anyone with my database platform as long as I had a name and an address. You had to in my line of work.

When you provide security for people like I did, it was always best to check up on them first.

For now though, now since I was all the way up here near the Port of Los Angeles I thought I should take a starboard tack on the bike and visit my old buddy Mack. He was probably on a shift down at the docks. He was always either on a shift or heading off of one. Four on and four off, he called them. Four hours of grinding dangerous work, and four hours off and you get paid for the whole eight hours. Go home, take a shower, get some sleep and then back to the union hall to pick up another shift. Two sixteen hour paid shifts per day, every day.

I texted him and he texted right back. He was heading off a shift and would meet me at the coffee shop near the south entrance to the docks.

I hadn't seen him for a year, but he hadn't changed one bit. When I walked into the busy restaurant, there he was at an inside table. It looked like he'd just devoured a plate of food and had a full cup of steaming coffee on the side. He mopped up the last of the potatoes and gravy with a corner of a bun, and saw me coming through the door, and waved me over.

"Badger, how you been?" He put me in a bear hug. His arms were like the thick end of a baseball bat with clubs on the end. Strong as an ox from working on the docks for twenty years. Half-Irish, half-Spanish he had black curly hair and freckles splayed over his nose and a twinkle in his blue eyes.

"Thought I'd take a ride on the bike," I said. "Get some fresh air. What's new on the docks?"

There was always something going on and I liked to hear the stories. The only problem was, once you got Mack going with 'what's going on the docks', you might never get him to stop. He'd been a big drinker in the past, got in trouble, almost lost everything, but that was in the past. He hadn't had a drink in years and was a cold sober worker now. From an alcoholic to a workaholic.

"See that guy over there?" And he pointed to a sharp dressed black guy heading to his car, a bright red Ferrari parked in the lot. "That's Chuck, cool guy, one of the regular bosses. He works every overtime shift he can get, been on the docks for over forty years, probably pulls in five hundred grand a year."

He took a sip of his coffee. "Let me buy you lunch."

"Naw I'm good."

"You sure?"

"Just coffee."

And he waved at the waitress who was buried in order-taking a couple of tables down, pointed at the coffee in his hand and then at me and winked at her, and she winked back.

"That's how we do it on the docks, Badger. When we're down in the hold of the ship and we give the crane driver a signal and he's about five hundred feet up in the air, he damn well better be able to tell what we're trying to convey to him. Some of those containers weigh over a hundred thousand pounds and you don't want to get your signals mixed up and get crushed, you know what I mean."

"How's the port these days, busy?"

"You kidding me? It's non-stop. I just got off a four-hour shift and I'm heading back on in four hours for the night shift. I gotta go back to the union hall and pick up my job slip, I might get elevated to boss. We're disembarking a ship from Taiwan, it's got two thousand containers and we'll be done by tomorrow night sometime and then it'll head up to San Francisco and Seattle before going back to Singapore for another load. You see, they bring their product here and dump it, and we send them our product back as trade using the same vessel. Have to keep the ships busy one way and the other, don't want to waste fuel, you know. Only problem is the load from our side that goes back over to China is usually less than half what we got coming here. It's a trade imbalance and we see it first-hand here on the docks. But at least we're busy, you know what I'm saying Badger? We're not the guys making the rules, we're just the workers."

"How's security these days? How do they know what's in all those containers?"

"I'll tell you, homeland security is all over the place. You see when the ship gets close to the shore, they send out a tug boat and board the ship, check out the log, and secure the bridge, hook up the tugs and bring it ashore to the dock. This whole place is on lock down, no one gets in or out without clearance. Then when we start bringing the containers off, every single one of them goes through a scanner. If they see something wrong they take it to a secure area, bust the lock and search the whole thing from top to bottom. They don't mess around, I'm telling you."

He took a sip of coffee and kept going. Man this guy could talk.

"Last week, get this Badger, they found something when they were doing a scan, they pulled the container over to the side and put it in their secure area, it's all fenced with barbed wire and armed guards, and they left it for the night. Sometime before dawn, a bunch of guys with guns showed up with a truck, broke into the area, held up the guards, tied them up and drove off with the container. They never found it."

"What was in it?" I asked.

He shrugged his shoulders. "It could have been full of weapons, drugs, we never found out, and they never told us. They run their show and we run ours. Just another day on the docks, you know what I mean? So what have you been up to Badge, how's the protection racket going?"

I told him about finding the girl off the coast of Catalina yesterday, the money and I.D. in the bag. The fake address.

He listened thoughtfully as I told him the whole sordid story from finding her in the water and turning her over to the Coast Guard, to visiting the house listed on her driver's license and finding out that she didn't live there and never had.

When I finished he shrugged his shoulders. "You say she looked Chinese?"

"Pretty much."

"Smugglers," he said simply.

"Really?"

"That's my guess. And I'll tell you what, it's not even a guess, I would bet a week's wages on it, and that's a lot of money where I work. Somebody was smuggling a bunch of Chinese in a boat and she fell overboard, simple as that. Or, maybe the whole boat capsized or sank and there's a lot more of them out there."

"That's what I was worried about," I said. "That there was more out there."

"But you only found one right?"

"So far."

"A hundred percent chance that it was a smuggling operation, and fifty-fifty that she fell overboard."

"Smugglers?"

"It's happening all the time Badger. Not too long ago we unloaded a giant ship from China, we had a container on the docks and when they scanned it they didn't find anything wrong, but later that night security came across a dozen Chinese guys trying to get out through the fence. Trying to get out, understand? Turns out they were living in one of the cargo containers when it was shipped from China and it had some trap doors built in so they could escape when the time was right. They rounded them up and took them to a detention center where they probably claimed asylum and are running a restaurant now somewhere in the city."

I thought about my buddy running his restaurant down in La Brea. "A Chinese guy saved me one time," I said.

Mack shrugged. "Hey, they're good workers don't get me wrong. Just knock on the front door for crying out loud and ask permission to come in, don't break in through the back and sneak in, you know what I'm saying?"

I nodded. "So it's happening all the time you say? You know this for a fact?"

"That's just one story. A couple of years ago a ship with over two hundred came close to San Francisco and they tried to ferry them to shore using legitimate local fishing boats thinking no one would notice. They busted 'em as soon as they set foot on land. The Coast

Guard was tracking them the whole time. And there was the time a ship carrying over three hundred of 'em ran aground in Santa Barbara. They just ran that ship right up onto the beach and all the illegals jumped off the ship. They'll try anything Badger. And it's big money too. The guys from the San Francisco deal said they paid fifty thousand each for the ride over. There were two hundred of 'em. That's ten million in cash. That's some serious money, Badger."

"Yeah." I sipped my coffee and mused the possibilities. I could fit ten Chinese guys on the Sugar, sail them over from Shanghai and pocket half a million per trip. It'd probably take a month round trip. Half a million a month, six million per year. In five years I'd have thirty million in the bank and I could retire. "Where do I sign up?" I asked.

"What?"

"Yeah, how do I sign up to be a smuggler?"

He laughed. "There's no union hall Badger. You can't just walk in and get a job slip and go to work. These guys are all underground, and dangerous too I'd imagine."

"I'll just sail over to mainland China, dock at some port and put the word on the street that I'm running a route."

"They'll chop your head off in some back alley and take your boat, re-paint it and put a new name on it. Think about how tight and militarized China is, Badger. That place is like a prison for most people, they don't get out unless the authorities let them out. If they try

BILL THESKEN

to escape and get caught they get chained to a rice paddy for the rest of their lives. Now think about the organized crime guys that are smuggling these people out. If those guys get caught they get a single bullet in the head and buried in a ditch. They are probably the most ruthless killers you've ever seen." And then he stopped and smiled and shook his head. He knew the details of some of the adventures I'd been on in the streets of L.A, and abroad. "Well, maybe the top ten percent of ruthless killers *you've* ever seen. In fact, in light of some of the gangsters you've been up against, I'd say you're probably one of the few people that could start up a smuggling operation on your own. But don't, okay?"

I took another sip of coffee and shook my head. "What I don't get is how they come up with fifty thousand dollars each. That's a ton of money for anyone, but for a Chinese guy...."

"I was sort of wondering about that too," said Mack. "I think what happens is all the family members chip in to a big pot to get whoever they want to send over to the states in the hopes that maybe they'll get some of the money back when their guy starts working hard and sending it back in the mail."

"They probably pick the youngest strongest and smartest one who has the best chance of working two or three jobs. Get 'em over here, get them plugged in, have some kids who are instant citizens, and then try to get rest of them over the legal way."

"I don't think so, Badger. It's probably just

like in the old days, when these guys leave their families, they don't ever expect to see them again and vice versa. The family probably sacrifices everything they have to get this one person out so they can live a better life. You know what I'm saying? They sacrifice their lives for them, in a way."

I thought about Mei Young Lee, if that was even her name. What type of family she had that sacrificed everything to get her to America. Maybe they were waiting anxiously in some grimy town in China, waiting for word that she'd arrived safely. Waiting for a letter or a postcard or a phone call. Anything. Waiting in vain until the end of their days. Tormented by the unknown.

"I'm thinking about digging into this a little farther to see if I can find out where she came from."

"What are you now, the police, the FBI?"

"Just an interested third party."

"You dig into this too far and maybe you'll be digging your own grave. My advice is to walk away."

Funny, that's exactly what I told myself a couple of hours ago.

"I guess it's not in my nature."

"How in the hell are you going to dig into it anyways? She fell off a boat for crying out loud. I know you Indian guys like to follow the trail, use your instincts out in the woods to track your game, but in this case there is no trail. It's just an empty ocean."

"There's always a trail, if you know where

to look. This is a trail of people. I got a bad feeling when I was talking to the neighbor of the fake address. Something's wrong. I don't know what it is, and I don't think I can just let it go."

He sighed and shook his head. "Oh well. Your folks wanted to name you after an animal? They should have named you after a damned mule, cause you sure are as stubborn as one. Don't say I didn't warn you. So now what?"

"I'll call the coroner's office in Catalina, see if anyone claimed the body. She did have ten thousand in cash on her. Maybe someone knows that and wanted to make sure it got to the right place, if you know what I mean."

Maybe I could take a ride out to Chinatown, and poke around a little bit, visit my old buddy at the restaurant.

6.

I knew one bona-fide Chinese person that might be able to help, so I thought it would be best to go have a little chat, and rode the chopper up north to the border of Chinatown and downtown LA.

It had been nearly a year since I was there last and that was a frantic couple of days in my life, pursued by the police, the firm, and the mob. Shot off my motorcycle by a sniper and discovered by the nearby restaurant owner, broken and unconscious in the empty warehouse next door that I'd managed to crash into. And after that, running for my life for three hectic days and nights.

The street looked different. A lot nicer than what I'd remembered.

What had been a semi-ghetto, busted windows, graffiti on the walls, trash in the streets, abandoned cars, homeless junkies sleeping in the alleyways, was now a brand new gleaming showpiece of the inner city.

There was a boutique hotel with a doorman

and a grand columned entrance, a small movie theatre, stores, restaurants, flower shops. I think I actually smiled as I pulled in to a parking space, and looked at the street sign again to make sure I was in the right place. And there was the little Chinese restaurant, same little sign, same bent over little man sweeping the steps.

I smiled at him as I stood in front of the first step. "Are you open today?"

He turned and squinted at me with a perpetual smile. "Yes, yes, always open. Come in, come in." Then he pointed at me with a crooked finger and his smile doubled in size. He remembered me. "Aw you! Yes, yes, let me get the door for you!" And he hobbled up the steps and opened the screen door and waved me in, beaming.

The place was nearly full and loud, waiters and busboys hustling from table to table and you could hear flame searing chopping sounds coming from the kitchen in the back of the building, along with light wisps of smoke and wonderful sweet and sour smells.

I found an empty table by the front window, sat down and made myself comfortable.

A young Chinese man dressed in a suit came out of the back by the kitchen, gave an order to one of the wait-staff, and greeted a customer seated at a table, asking him how was the food, is there anything else they needed, and thank you for coming in. The owner of the restaurant, making the rounds. On his face was a perpetual smile, just like the old man sweeping the front steps.

He saw me sitting at the table by the front door, and the muscles in his face suddenly went slack, the warm ambiance draining out, replaced by cold dread. He walked towards me, trying to put the perpetual smile back on his face as he passed the tables, nodding to his customers as he walked, but I could see the square edges of his face tinged with doubt, and anger, and soon enough he was standing in front of me, his face turned away from all others in the room, so no-one could see the fire in his eyes.

The suit fit snugly and you couldn't see his body, but by the taught sinews of his fists, neck and cheekbones he gave the appearance of someone that it wouldn't pay to disagree with.

Unless you wanted a quick karate chop to the neck.

He tried to hide it with the long cuffs of his shirt, but I saw the edge of a tattoo above the inside of his wrist, Chinese lettering. He spoke softly so the people nearby couldn't hear him.

"What are you doing here?"

"I came for lunch."

"Bullshit."

"You don't look too happy to see me."

"Wherever you go, trouble follows, and I don't like trouble. I told you never to come back here. You don't listen, you never listen."

"I heard that people live longer if they smile."

"You might live longer if you leave now."

He made a fist with his right hand, which was hanging by his side. I could hear the knuckles crack.

"The street looks a hell of a lot better than it did the last time I was here. I heard the landlord passed away, and someone else who wasn't so ghetto-minded took over."

"I heard the landlord got pushed out of a window. By you."

"That's a lie, he tripped and fell out. But the result was the same."

"He tripped and fell out, huh?"

"Yeah, that's the truth. But if he didn't fall out, I was about to throw him out. He beat me to the punch. Ironic, isn't it?"

"So what do you want?"

"How about a plate of sweet sour pork and rice."

"I mean what do you want from me."

"Business looks good." I waved my hand to the full-capacity room.

"Yeah, it's good, very good in fact, and I want it to stay that way, with no trouble following you through that door."

"Look Wang..."

"How'd you know my name?"

When we first met he wouldn't tell me his name, so I looked into it.

"Your name is Wang lei. In Chinese it means a pile of rocks. In my line of work you can find out anything about anyone, and most of the time it's a good practice. You saved me, and I saved you, in a way, saved your business, life is good now for both of us. What do you say, let's forget the past for now and just look towards the future as friends."

"I don't need friends."

"Well I do. Please sit down for a moment." And I pointed to the empty chair opposite from me. "Please," I repeated.

He sighed and shook his head and sat down, resigned to the fact that I wasn't going to go away until I got what I wanted. He waved to one of the waiters to bring water and spread his hands on the table, palms up, in the universal gesture of 'let's get on with this'.

"I need your advice."

His face remained still. "Okay."

The waiter brought two glasses of ice water and set them in front of us. Wang nodded in thanks and waved him off.

"I'll level with you. Yesterday when I was sailing off the north coast of Catalina Island I found the body of a young woman, floating in the ocean. She looked Chinese, had a Chinese name, and a driver's license with an address in Long Beach that was fake."

He sighed heavily and rubbed the deep lines on his forehead with his hand for a moment. "I knew this was trouble. How do you know it was fake."

"The guy living next door said she never lived there."

"Maybe he was lying."

"I considered that. She was also carrying about ten thousand in cash."

His face remained stoic, and then he leaned forward half an inch.

"Maybe she was going shopping on a cruise liner when she fell overboard, or maybe she was swimming and hit her head on a rock and just happened to have a little extra cash on hand, it made her feel better just having it nearby. You're a racist American, you probably think all Chinese people love money right?"

"Well don't you?"

He shrugged his shoulders and I continued.

"My buddy who works at the docks says that she was probably being smuggled into the country."

"Don't be naïve Badger. If it looks like a dog and barks like a dog, it's probably a dog."

"That's why I'm here."

"Don't tell me it's because I'm Chinese."

"You're a tight knit community. It's a well-known fact that you stick together, and look after each other, that's why you thrive."

"We're a tight knit community, but we thrive because we mind our own business, which is what you should learn to do."

"I can't just let this go."

"What, are you a cop now?"

"I'm not a cop."

"You ask questions like a cop."

"I'm just trying to get some answers so I can sleep at night."

"I know where this is heading. You asked me for my advice, and my advice to you right now is to walk away from this as fast as you can."

I looked around at the restaurant. It was

nearly packed, and loud.

"You have a busy establishment. You have a lot of workers."

"And they all look Chinese, so maybe they're illegal right? Maybe we smuggled them in? Well my friend, they're all documented, I can tell you that for a fact."

"I told you I'm not a cop, I don't care if they're documented or not."

"Well you're going to hear it anyways. Some of them are straight from mainland China, and some are from Taiwan, and if for some reason they weren't documented, I'd find a way to get the process started, and protect them. People need to work, they need to eat and have a place to live. It's a basic human right."

"Fair enough, so if one of them should God forbid perish, wouldn't you want their family to know about it?"

"Sure, I'd call them on the phone and take care of all the arrangements. These workers are like family to me, and we take care of our own."

"Maybe you're right, maybe she did fall off a cruise liner, and in that case she'll be reported missing. But just hypothetically speaking, what if she was being smuggled into the country, how do we find out her true identity, and let her family know what happened to her?"

"What am I, the Chinese missing persons bureau?"

"You're a tight knit community. You said it

yourself. I just want to know who's doing the smuggling."

He leaned forward and his voice got smaller, nearly a whisper. "You're going to get yourself killed. The people who do the smuggling are not the type of people you want to mess with. Stop asking questions, and walk away. Why do you care anyways? What's in it for you?"

"For some reason I'm the guy who found her. Aren't you a mystical Kung Fu guy? I saw the tattoo, I know what you've been through to get that. I've been through some of your training. I know the mindset that goes with it. You know that we're all connected in this world somehow, and nothing is by accident. I found her for a reason, and I don't know what that reason is yet."

The edges of his face got tighter and he spoke through gritted teeth. "Maybe the reason is that you are a dumb ass, who needs to mind his own business."

He sighed heavily and shook his head. It was like he was beating a dead horse.

"Look, you know that people are being smuggled into this country every hour of every day, and you don't have to be a genius to know why. The people that do the smuggling are ruthless, it could be anyone, the Triads, the Mexican Mafia, Russian Mafia. There's big money involved and they don't want anyone stepping on their toes."

He took a sip of water and narrowed his eyes, looking around first to make sure no one could listen to what he was about to say, and then leaning closer, speaking even softer.

"But the fact remains that if she is Chinese, and she was being smuggled, then it is the Triad, for they are the most ruthless of them all, and none of the other players want to mix it up with them, or take their business. And that is even more of a reason for you to walk away. You're just one man, you don't have a chance against them if you piss them off."

I nodded. "Okay, you make a good argument. And that's why I wanted to talk to you first. I'll take your advice. I'll take a step back and just monitor the situation and stay out of it."

He finally smiled. "Now you're talking."

"I'll just call over to the island now and then, and see if anyone claimed the body."

His smile faded, his mouth went slack, while his eyes turned dull.

"I could punch you in the face right now, but I'd probably break my fist because your entire head must be made out of cement."

7.

Two o'clock in the afternoon was the busiest time of the day at the recreation center and park in the northern corner of Chinatown. An elementary school sat right across the street, two blocks away running east to west was Chavez Ravine, and rising on the hill beyond the ravine was the mighty Dodger Stadium.

When there's an afternoon game and the Santa Ana winds are blowing from the mountains to the sea, you can hear the crack of the bat on the ball and the crowd roaring, but today was an off day and most of the ambient noise came from the cars on the street.

Packs of kids both large and small, chattering, laughing and running, fresh out of school carrying backpacks and books, were making their way home in herds, some stopping at the basketball court to shoot hoops while others gathered at the playground to play on the jungle gym and slides.

An impeccably dressed middle-aged man

sat on the end of the park bench reading the Chinese language newspaper, from back to front, while listening to the commotion around him. The busier it was, the better. He'd been sitting there for ten minutes. He glanced at his watch, noting it was the exact time of the planned meeting, then looked over the top of the paper to see a stout Caucasian man in a black windbreaker with close cropped hair walking his way, not paying attention to anything in particular, not in a hurry. He stopped to watch the basketball game for a moment and smiled as one of the players scored on a long jump shot, then he continued on his way and stopped near the bench.

"Mind if I sit down?" The man motioned on the other end of the bench.

"Not at all, please do."

They did not look at each other again. The Chinese man kept reading his paper, while the stout man studied the park and all the activity.

Then they began speaking in Mandarin in low tones to each other with the Chinese man speaking first.

"You lost a package on the last mission."

"Yes. It was our first loss."

"The organizers are not happy. The girl was on her way to an arranged marriage with a very important man."

"We can't undo what has happened."

"Yes, that is true."

"Will they be able to find a replacement bride?"

"Perhaps, everything is replaceable."

The implication was direct.

"Do we still have your confidence?"

"Mine, yes. The organizers, maybe not."

"So what now?"

"They need to make up for their loss."

"How?"

"They wish to include some packages that cannot speak."

"You know we can't do that."

"You have an arrangement within your team that will not allow it."

"You know that is true."

"Then re-arrange your team."

"You also know it's not that simple."

"Nothing is easy. Remember when we first met? You were an attaché with the US Army in Beijing. And I was your exact opposite in the Chinese Red Army."

"Yes, that was a long time ago."

"You managed to re-arrange your position, to what you are today. And I have done the same. Anything is possible."

"Some things are more possible than others. Changing someone's moral position is sometimes impossible, if they are set in their ways. Our team-mate is set in his convictions and we need him on our team. We cannot transport drugs. Only people."

"Maybe he'll decide to leave the team."

"It's possible, but only if it's his choice, and not forced upon him. I won't have it any other way. I'll try to convince him to accept your offer. But I can't make any guarantees."

"You know him well."

"Since we were in diapers."

"Please keep trying. Their patience is wearing thin, and we may have to find a new route. Some things are out of my control."

"I understand. When is our next shipment?"

"Soon, I will let you know well in advance."

"There's something else."

"What."

"The man who found the body came to the house asking questions."

"So?"

"I'm not sure. Something about him doesn't seem right. He must have seen the address on her driver's license and either memorized it, or wrote it down. When I told him no Chinese girl had ever lived in the house, and he probably made a mistake with the street name, he agreed too quickly, and left immediately after. We did some research and found out where he lives, in Dana Point on his boat. He runs a personal security firm. I have no doubt that he's ex-military."

"Do you want us to take care of the situation?"

"I'll handle it."

"Remember," said the Chinese man. "The strongest and most expensive robe in the world can unravel with a single loose thread." Then he folded the front page of the paper he was reading into the main bulk of the newspaper and set it on the bench between them, rose to his feet, and walked off.

The stout man waited a few minutes,

seemingly enjoying the sunshine and fresh air, then picked up the paper and walked in the other direction. He could feel the stack of money in the middle of the paper, and smiled as he walked.

8.

I rode the chopper back to the harbor, taking my time in the slow lane, passing through the sprawling beachside towns of Huntington, ~~and~~ Newport, and Laguna. I revved the engine at pretty girls and kids, getting worried looks from half the people who saw me and all the old ladies, except for one, an old ex-biker chick that looked like she was in her late seventies. She was mostly skin and bones, weathered tattoos and attitude, wearing a leather jacket with the sleeves cut off, smoking a cigarette while sitting on the stone wall next to the basketball courts in Laguna.

She flipped me the bird as she saw me coming down the highway, with a big toothless grin and then put her thumb high in the air to try and hitch a ride.

"Good for her," I thought, but I shook my head and revved the engine a little louder for her as I passed by. I could see the glint in her eyes and I knew that fifty years ago she wouldn't have needed to hitchhike and beg for a ride, she probably would have had them lined up and down the road just begging for her to hop on the back. That's the way of the world. The older you got the less opportunities were afforded to you and the harder life was.

My Dad had a saying, he'd pull it out of his endless stockpile of advice and tell it to me once in a while when he could sense that I getting lazy, taking things for granted, not trying with all my might.

"Son," he'd say, "we're not going to be here forever, that we should know without the shadow of a doubt. But we're here right now, so we might as well make the most of it while we can."

And if you thought about it, that old dried up ex-biker chick sitting on the wall trying to hitch a ride and re-capture a bit of her youth was like a poster child for that statement. We're here now, so never give up.

I headed up and over the hill past the million dollar suburbia that stretched to the south of Laguna, then stopped along the cliff that led down to Dana Point to watch the beginnings of the sunset in the west.

The sky was just starting to show a bit of red and orange on the edges and the old wives tale of "red sky at night sailors delight" came to mind. It actually did look like it would be a good day for sailing tomorrow, with moderate winds and calm seas. Red sky at night be damned.

Amber was working a double shift at the hospital and would only be wanting sleep and quiet time after clocking out tomorrow morning, so there was no sense in me getting in the way. Plus I needed to research the problem at hand, and my computer set-up on the Spice was the best money could buy.

In essence, a basic internet connection could get you just about all the intel you needed to get by in life, but I needed an extra dose of semi-secret inside info with software that was housed on my computer.

Now that I was a one man operation in charge of every aspect of the business, I needed to cover all the bases for protecting the client. I made a business decision right off the bat that if I was going to put my life on the line to protect someone, even if it was only for a couple of hours, I was going to know everything about that person, good bad happy or sad, every tiny scrap of detail that might get us both killed, or save us.

With my data mining software I could pull up all the dirty details on anyone, from the King of Arabia to the guy picking up the trash at four in the morning. Any lawsuit, traffic ticket, parking fine, returned check, social media smack talking confrontations, even their medical and dental and school records all the way back to pre-school and the hospital they were born in.

I would get a snapshot of their lives in an easy to read, two-page, seven hundred word synopsis. Within twenty minutes I would know more about someone than their spouse or parent. I would know more about them than they knew about themselves. After all, who has access to their school records or has even seen what is hidden in the principal's files? I would know things they wanted to forget and maybe in fact had forgotten on purpose.

If someone was out to get my client and my client didn't want to tell me about it, there could be a problem, so I absolutely did not want to leave it up to the client to inform me. My motto is: trust no one, ever.

Except Amber. She was the one person in this whole world that I trusted completely. It was funny how I was lucky enough to find a girl like her. Smart, beautiful, could make a nice meal, and could set a broken bone or sew up a knife wound in a snap.

I fired up the chopper, continued down to the harbor, turned in at the entrance, and motored past lines and lines of tethered boats towards my two moorings. The Spice was sitting solid and upright at her berth, but the Sugar was listing, the mast tilting at a seventy degree angle towards the sunset. I gunned the engine to get there quick.

Two people were standing on the dock looking at the sailboat, one of them looked like he was getting ready to jump aboard her when he heard the sound of the motorcycle, and looked towards me, and waited. It was Tom, the harbor master. I slammed on the brakes next to the boat and jumped off the bike.

"Looks like she's taking on water," shouted the harbor master. "Your neighbor here called me and I came right over."

It was listing away from the dock and the port side was lifted up. There was an eight-foot gap between the dock and the deck. I jumped up onto the side of the boat, grabbed the railing, pulled myself up, and climbed aboard. I pulled a small flashlight out of my pocket and pointed it down into the hatch that was busted open. Water was up to the bunk beds and three-feet deep on the floor.

I yelled to the dock.

"Get a portable pump right away, I'm going to try to get the bilge pump started!"

I didn't wait to see their response. I jumped down in the cockpit, crawled into the cabin, and was instantly waste deep in the water.

There's an alarm on the bilge pump and if water is entering the hull it automatically turns itself on and pumps it out. It also sets off a loud alarm that can heard miles away. It has obviously malfunctioned and if I didn't act fast, the boat would list farther on its side, water would gush into the open cockpit, and she will sink like a rock.

I opened a side panel and took out a snorkel, mask, and a large waterproof flashlight, then moved forward into the dark cabin. I turned on the flashlight and put on the diving mask, then I reached down into the water and pulled the hatch cover that led to the interior of the hull.

The submersible bilge pump was located right on the bottom of the hull, and is about the size of large toaster, and I would see through the water that the power switch is off. Somehow the water was entering the hull. I swung the beam of light along the surface. There was an intake valve on the hull attached to a pipe system that brings water in to the toilet flushing system. The pipe had been broken off and water must have been gushing through that hole.

Lucky thing I've also trained for this scenario.

Every boat should have a couple of tins of emergency leak sealant, and mine was stowed right underneath the bunk in case I need to grab it in the middle of the night mid channel.

It's like a putty, sticky and gooey and would have come in handy for the little Dutch boy who put his finger in the dike. I molded a baseball-sized bunch in my hand, took a deep breath and dove to the bottom of the hull. I pushed it into the hole, jamming it in with the palm of my hand until I was certain it was snug on all sides.

It was an epoxy-type material and the water was the catalyst, setting off a chemical chain reaction and firming the material within minutes.

While I was down there I pushed the button on the side of the bilge pump and could hear it whirring to life. I rose back to the surface, inhaled and exhaled a couple of times, then took another deep breath and went back down to investigate.

I shone the light on the intake valve, there were markings like the teeth from a pair of pliers. Someone must have climbed down here, turned off the bilge pump, and ripped the intake valve off with a pair of pliers. They tried to sink the Sugar.

I rose back to the surface, hopped on the deck, and looked over the side where I could see water gushing from ~~of~~ the out-take valve high on the hull, halfway down the boat.

The bilge pump had a flow rate of five hundred gallons an hour which seemed like a lot but was only a little over eight gallons per minute. There was probably a thousand gallons down in the hull.

The harbor masters truck came roaring up. ~~and~~ He jumped out and pulled a big pump from the back.

He set it on the dock, fired up the gas engine, and threw the hose up to me. I snaked it first down into the cabin and then further through the hatch to the bottom of the hull.

His pump was for serious situations, like raising a boat that was half sunk, mine was for little leaks, that were never supposed to get that far. And it wouldn't have gotten that far if it was turned on, if it had turned on like it was designed.

Someone tried to sink my boat. Now why in the hell would someone do that?

It took a little over half an hour to suck all the water out. I mopped up the remaining puddles with a large sponge and a bucket, checked all the electrical circuits with a multimeter and re-hooked up the wiring to the bilge pump. Then I tested it again to make sure it was working.

Tom coiled the hose from his pump, loaded

it back on his truck, and hopped back aboard the Sugar.

"That was close," he said.

"Yeah."

"You think it was deliberate?"

"I do."

"I'll put in a call to the police."

"Not yet."

"Why not?"

"I want to do some investigating on my own first, if that's okay."

"I don't know Badger, it's pretty standard operating procedure that if a crime has been committed in a harbor, which is federal juris-diction, that we call in the coast guard and the police. I've got my job on the line."

"You have surveillance cameras right?"

"Sure, there's one at the entrance, and one above the harbor master's office, but not one that covers the whole harbor and every boat in it, not yet anyways, it's in the budget as a future expense."

"Can we take a look at the feed before you call anybody?"

He thought about it for a minute, his face concerned, biting his lip, then relented.

"Okay. We'll do it your way."

We jumped in his truck and drove the short distance to the harbor master's office, a one-story square building with his office on the end.

At his desk he turned on his computer, rolled over an icon on the screen and clicked on it. A TV image came up that was right outside the office and looking down the ramp towards where the Sugar was berthed.

"You see we can't actually see your boat with this camera."

"What about the entrance to the harbor?"

"Sure," he said and clicked on another link. On this video we could see the gated entrance, with cars arriving and leaving.

"Can you make it split screen so we see both at the same time?"

"Yep, say you know how these systems work don't you?"

"I've been shopping around for one, I was supposed to get one for my boats, I guess kind of like the government, it's in the budget as future expense. I just haven't gotten around to it yet."

"So this is the live view."

"How long ago do you think the boat got the leak?"

"I'm thinking half an hour before I got here, and it took half an hour to pump the water out, so let's scroll back an hour and see what we find."

At the bottom of the screen was a play button and an arrow at the end of a line. Tom clicked on the arrow and dragged it backwards, the scene on the screen turning crazy as people and cars moved in reverse.

Quite a few people walked down to the area where the Sugar was berthed, but one character in particular caught our attention.

"Check this guy out with the hoodie. He heads down towards the Sugar, and about five minutes later he heads back this way. But check out his face."

"Yeah we can't see it." The guy had the hoodie bunched tight and tied off, covering his forehead, cheeks, and chin, and he was wearing dark sunglasses.

"Looks like a pretty big guy, don't you think?"

"Tough to say with that bulky sweatshirt, but yeah he seems to fill it out pretty good. Take a look at that big, wide nose of his. Those don't fit on skinny guys."

"What was he driving when he came in?"

Tom kept moving the footage forward and he pointed to the screen that showed the entrance. "There he is, walking up and out. He didn't drive in."

There were cars parked up and down the street outside the entrance.

"Keep it rolling."

"If that's our guy, then he's pretty smart and knows the lay-out of the harbor, knows not to drive in and out so we can see his license plate number."

The guy kept walking across the street then took a left turn, walked a few cars down and got into the driver's side of a vehicle parked on the other side of the road.

"Stop the footage right here, and zoom in."

"You can't see what kind of car it is with the chain link fence in the way."

Tom zoomed in until the outline of the top of a truck showed through the chain-link. The picture was fuzzy, but they got an idea of what it was.

"Looks like a white or a silver truck. Big one."

"Yeah."

"Know the guy?"

"I got a hunch. Go ahead and call the cops or the Coast Guard, Tom. Do whatever you have to do. I'm gonna take a ride."

"This isn't much to go on Badger. We can't tell if the guy went to your boat or not, we can't see his face, and we can't tell what kind of truck he got into. He looks like a suspicious dude though."

I jumped on the bike, fired it up, and gunned through Dana Point to the freeway on-ramp and into the fast lane. I got my speed up to a steady seventy-five sometimes eighty miles an hour, and within thirty minutes I was back at Belmont Shores with my spyglass trained on my new best friends' house.

The garage door was closed, but the large silver truck was on the outside. The engine was running, I could see a small stream of white exhaust leaving the tailpipe, and wisping into the air.

Jack came out of the house carrying a large square briefcase. He slammed the front door hard and jumped in the driver's side of the truck, backed out of the driveway, and raced off.

I followed far behind. He zigzagged the three miles through the afternoon traffic towards Long Beach Harbor and parked in the lot next to the Catalina ferry.

I parked a block away, my bike hidden by a

row of cars, and watched through the scope.

It was five-thirty in the afternoon and the crew was nearly done boarding the ship, getting ready to shove off for their last trip of the day.

Jack half-ran, half-jogged toward the ramp and showed the two agents at the gate a ticket. They smiled, slapped him on the back, and talked for a bit. I took three things from watching.

They were friendly.

They knew each other.

This wasn't the first time he'd been on the ferry to Catalina.

9.

I decided to take a ride back over to 'ol Jack Wilson's house, wait for it to get dark, and poke around a little bit. See who I was really dealing with.

I parked by the harbor and watched the sun slowly melt into the horizon, a red ball sinking into a dark vat of smog and salt spray.

Off in the distance you could hear a tugboat's mournful horn as it entered Long Beach harbor escorting another giant container ship. With the sun well below the horizon now and the land temperature dropping, the wind turned from on-shore to off-shore, and the smell of the wind turned from salt spray and kelp to ozone.

I could see Jack's house from my seat on the bike. All the streets had underground utilities and with no lines leading to the roof line, I couldn't spot where the electric meter was hooked up to the house. I took out my scope and pinpointed the breaker box on the other side of a short brick wall next to the garage.

When it was nearly pitch black I took a little walk.

It was guaranteed he'd have motion activated perimeter lighting, and an alarm system for the interior of the house, so I'd have to work fast.

The way I figured it, all I really needed was three minutes. I didn't have to find out everything about this guy right now, I just needed a little snapshot. Some pictures on the wall, what's in the fridge, the medicine cabinet, the top drawer of his desk. Three minutes, and if the alarm went off I could be in and out long before the cops got there to ask me what I was doing.

The street was quiet and deserted, everyone nearby had either gone out to eat, or was inside having dinner and watching TV. No one sitting on their front porch, no one walking their dog. No one looking out of their windows.

I angled in along the driveway, walking normal, not fast or running, just another resident out for an evening stroll. When I got within ten feet of the house, the light on the front of the garage door lit up. I jumped over the fence, opened up the breaker box, pulled out my taser, put it next to the main switch, and pulled the trigger. A blue bolt of current from the taser fried the main breaker and sent a little surge through the house electrical system, knocking out the perimeter light, all the breakers in the house, and hopefully the interior security system.

You never could be completely certain about

these things. Usually the system ran strictly on direct current power, but sometimes it was rigged as a dual system, wired to the house electrical grid and with a battery back-up in case of a power outage.

Five minutes. That's all I needed and the clock was running. Time for some old fashioned B and E.

Breaking and entering.

There was a row of French style windows waist-high on the side of the house. I picked out the closest one, and with my gloved fist, punched out a little square frame of glass.

That is why they call it breaking and entering, first you break the window, and then you enter.

Reaching up I unlatched the window, pulled it up, and climbed in. No alarm yet, no alarm that I could hear, that is. They could always have a silent alarm, they were actually the best, get the thief to relax, stick around long enough for the authorities to show up and put some metal brackets on their wrists.

I went quickly through the house, shining the red flashlight on all the walls in the living room, sweeping through the kitchen, looking in the cabinets and the refrigerator, there was a lot of frozen meat and dark beer, then finding the stairway to the second floor.

Three steps at time, I scanned the master bedroom, looked in the drawers, the closets, the bathroom and the medicine cabinet.

He had the usual items: aspirin, mouthwash, toothpaste, and wha-da-ya-know, a bottle of human growth hormone, anabolic steroids, and a little clear bottle full of little pills of prescription methamphetamine. My new best friend was a muscle and meth junkie.

There was a small handgun in the top drawer of the bedside table, and a sawed off double barreled shotgun under the bed. This guy was ready for action.

I swept through to the second bedroom. It had a couple of single beds and an empty closet. I got out of there quickly.

A third bedroom had the door shut, I carefully opened it. Looked like a typical home office with a desk, computer, printer, shredder... and another handgun in the top drawer. Not so typical.

The walls were filled with framed photographs, I looked quickly and carefully at each of them.

They must have been sentimental, keeping all these photos on the wall where he could look at them now and then, and not locked away in some cabinet.

Events, awards, hunting trips with big guys in safari hats kneeling down next to large dead animals, holding up lines of little fish, and one photo of a big black marlin on a hook next to a yacht in Hawaii.

Must have been a fishing tournament, since there was a pretty native girl wearing a colorful lei and a bright smile, and not much else, on the other side of the fish. A chalkboard above the harpoon read nine hundred fifty-five pounds. Not bad.

Off in the corner at the end of the wall was a small photo. It looked like one of the oldest ones of the bunch, the paper faded and brown with age. Jack Wilson in his younger days, looking very serious and standing on a great big brick lined avenue on top of a wall with a couple of serious looking Chinese dudes.

He was standing on the Great Wall of China as a matter of fact. I could see the massive structure winding off into the distance like a giant castle wall.

I studied the faces. There were two Asian guys standing on either side of Jack. They all looked to be in their early twenties at most.

Slim, tall, rigid framed, square shouldered, and stone faced. Now why in world, I wondered, were they so unsmiling and grim faced? Guys in their twenties were naturally like this, I knew, but this was over the top.

And then it hit me. They were grim faced because they were military. I knew it. I also knew that my three minutes was up, and I needed to get the heck out of there.

Down the dark stairs, out the open window on the side and crouching by the wall next to the garage, I peered over the side. Now, of all times, an old lady was walking her dog, and coming my way.

She was carrying a little plastic bag in case the dog does its business. She was a fairly old lady, walking a little crooked with frazzled gray hair and a dark overcoat. The dog stopped next to Jack's mailbox, sniffed around it, and then crouched over, leaving a small load.

"C'mon lady," I whisper. "Pick it up and get the heck out of here so I can leave." But she didn't pick it up. She looked around a bit, turning her head this way and that to see if anyone was watching. Satisfied that no one saw the dirty deed, she turned around and headed right back down the street the way she came.

I could almost see a little smile on her face.

She was carrying the plastic bag as a decoy, never intending to pick it up in the first place.

Brought her dog up here to leave Jack a present. I shook my head in dismay. You can't trust anyone these days.

10.

It was a ritual they started in the very beginning when they were young and none of them had a dime to their names. They sat around the big square table in the clubhouse and waited until everyone had an unopened beer and an envelope in front of them. All four of them, Don, Jack, Corbin, and Kyle.

The clubhouse had redwood paneled walls, a sand floor, and a tiny sliver view of the blue harbor at Avalon. Assorted trophies lined the walls, sailing races, swim races, surf contests, jujitsu, karate, skeet shooting.

There was also a monkey pod bar imported from Hawaii just last year, a slab cut from a single eight foot wide tree, the jagged irregular edges still intact with bark while the top surface was oiled and vibrant with the colors of the dark brown grain.

A pool table filled the remainder of the room, and a wide screen TV hung on the wall, next to photographs of races and contests and award ceremonies. It's was their sports cave, a shrine, of sorts, and a testament to past deeds of glory.

The clubhouse was a far cry nicer than the discarded wood and cardboard shack they built on the hill overlooking Avalon Bay when they were all kids, set into a hedge of cactus and shrub brush with a dirt floor and rocks for chairs.

"All set?" asked Don, and when they all nodded he twisted opened his beer and toasted them. "Here's to you and here's to me, and if we ever disagree, then screw you and here's to me."

"Hip hip," said Corbin, and they all opened their beers and envelopes, took long drinks and started counting the bills.

Each letter sized envelope had exactly four hundred and fifty Benjamin Franklins, crisp one hundred dollar bills stacked neatly in an inch thick bundle, and bound with a thick rubber band, and each man counted their personal stack carefully and silently, some of them stopping now and then to take a swig of beer.

Forty-five thousand per man.

Kyle finished counting first. "I'm five thousand short."

"How much you got?" asked Jack.

"Forty-five thousand."

"That's the take," said Jack.

"Supposed to be fifty."

"Should have been fifty," said Jack. "Except you lost one of the packages. Get out your calculator, ten packages, twenty grand each equals two hundred thousand. Divided by the four of us equals fifty grand."

"That's my point."

"Except you lost one of the packages. We lost twenty grand which divided by the four of us equals five grand each. Fifty minus five equals forty five all day long. You want me to get a calculator for you?"

"I didn't lose the package. Butterfingers over here lost the package." And Kyle pointed across the table at Corbin.

Corbin stared back at him. "Didn't anyone tell you it's not nice to point?"

"You lost the package. You cost us money."

Corbin threw his envelope on the table, his face beet red. "Don't give me that crap. We went over this already, we're in this together, one for all and all for one, like the four musketeers right? Like a team, we win as a team, and we lose as a team. We lost a package so we split the cost."

Kyle kept it up. "You were on the starboard side. That was your responsibility. You couldn't pull her in and now I'm short five grand. I got bills to pay you know."

"You got bills to pay? YOU GOT BILLS TO PAY? Keep it up and you're gonna have some hospital bills to pay asshole!"

Corbin slid out of his chair and kicked it clear, clenched his fists, crouched low and was ready to jump over the table at Kyle who also got up and stood ready, veins sticking out of their arms and necks.

At six-foot five and two hundred and fifty

pounds of lean muscle, a black belt in karate who could break a cinder block in half with his fist, Corbin was used to pushing his weight around wherever and whenever he wanted.

Smaller in size but also a black belt in Jiu-jitsu, Kyle avoided fighting, but was an expert grappler and could submit an orangutan with a choke hold.

"Maybe we should see which art form is the best?" said Corbin, and he started to circle around the table to his right. Kyle smiled and motioned with his hand to bring it on.

"Alright enough!" shouted Don and slammed his palm on the table. The two combatants slowly settled back into their chairs. "Shit happens right? First one we lost in a couple of years. We absorb the cost together, that's our deal." Don looked at Kyle. "It's only five grand, you worked ten days last year and made half a million bucks. Let it go."

"It's the principal," said Kyle.

"I had my hand on her," said Corbin. "And then that asshole Chinese dude panicked, thought he was gonna drown or get left behind and he climbed right the hell over her, used her like a damn ladder, just stepped right on top of her head and shoulders to get in the boat. Then he's grabbing onto me like a crab on the rocks, and I'm thinking he's gonna pull me over the side. I had to knock him in the jaw and drag him on the boat, the way he was scrambling he probably kicked her in the head and knocked her out, she gets pushed under water, and probably went under the starboard hull of the boat before she surfaced again. Or maybe way out the back I don't know, I never saw her again. A rogue wave hits the boat, people are screaming and yelling in Chinese. That was the worst drop we ever had." He took a long drink of his beer, then let out a sigh.

"She had to have been knocked out, unconscious," said Kyle. "And floated away, otherwise she would have yelled out and we could have found her. I'm the captain and it's ultimately my responsibility for the ship, the crew, and our passengers. Once we got everyone calmed down, I made our count and found out we had nine instead of ten. But by then it was too late. We were drifting, she was drifting, and probably at odd angles to each other, since the wind and current were offset where we were. We were catching a bit of the wind and she was only in the current. We were calling out to her, but she was unconscious and unable to shout back to us, I couldn't turn on the engines until we were sure she wasn't near us. The sea was rough, no moon, we used the red beam searchlights but she never showed on the crests of the waves. If their lifeboat hadn't flipped in the first place, none of this would have happened. It wasn't any one person's fault. What's done is done."

"I should have thrown that Chinese dude overboard," said Corbin, "and made *him* swim to shore." He turned to Jack. "You see what's happening? You're throwing a wedge into our team. You tell Chang next time you see him that we want that twenty thousand, or I'm going to take it out of his hide."

"How you gonna do that?" said Kyle. "He never comes over here, and you haven't left the island in what, two years?"

Corbin leaned back, took a long sip of his beer and smiled. "I've got everything I need right here. And if I need something that's not here, I have it shipped, special order. Like that Russian babe, Svetlana. Straight from Stalingrad, right out of a catalogue. But I might make an exception to make a visit to that slant-eyed bastard. "

"You want me to tell Chang that you're going to come over to the mainland and take it out on his hide? Are you crazy, or just stupid?"

Corbin pointed his finger at Jack and spoke slowly. "Don't you ever say that to me again."

They all sat silently for a moment until Don tapped the table and spoke. "Alright back to business. So, you all know that a pleasure boater found the girl off the north side of the island two days later."

They all nodded and a few took sullen swigs of beer. It was depressing. They were all watermen; sailors, swimmers, surfers and to lose someone to the ocean was a tragedy, business or no business, it was a life. They all knew that they were each holding a one-way ticket in this world, and it could be any one of them at any time, checking out and heading to the other side.

"What about the police investigation?" asked Kyle. "Any leads on how she went in the water?"

"The investigation is closed," said Don. "The coroner's office is reporting an unattended death by drowning, no head trauma, no foul play. The ID she was carrying is fake, so our determination is that she was being smuggled into the country and died in the attempt. We have no leads, no one has claimed the body, and no further investigation is necessary."

"However," said Jack. "We do have a bit of a situation." And they all looked over at him. "The guy who found her in the water is poking around, asking questions. He came to the fake address yesterday afternoon, said he was a friend of hers and that she told him to stop by sometime to visit her. He gave me a fake ass name, but we tracked him down. He called the Sheriff station this morning, looking for a status report, wanting to know if anyone claimed the body."

"Nosy bastard, isn't he?" said Kyle.

"What are we going to do about this guy?" asked Corbin.

"I took care of the problem."

"What does that mean?"

"I sent him a message, and I don't think we'll see him around here ever again. I sank his boat. We found out where he was moored, and I went down there and sank the bastard's boat, right at the dock."

They sat in silence watching him.

"It takes about ten seconds to open up the bilge pipe and bada bing."

"I don't like that," said Kyle. "You should

leave the guy's boat out of it."

"What if that just pisses him off?" asked Don.

"Then we'll take it up a notch" said Corbin with a grin. "And I'll get involved. But I'll sink his boat with him in it."

"I don't think he's going to be a problem," said Jack. "But if we do see him again, we'll have to deal with it, just like the last situation a few years ago. Another do-gooder snooping around, trying to find out where the Chinese tourists are coming from. This operation is worth five million a year to us, and we barely break a sweat. No one is going to get in the way I tell you, nobody. I'll make certain of that. Unless the other side takes care of it first."

"You remember that guy a couple of years ago, right?" continued Jack as he looked around the group. "Rented a room at the Inn for two months. Decided to do a survey on the ethnicity of tourists coming across on the ferries. Sat down there by the dock for a couple of weeks, all day, every day with a camera and a notepad and wrote down the creed and color of all the people coming off and going on when the boats came in, and when they left."

"He was a statistician," said Don. "Doing an independent study. Hoped he was gonna get a grant from the State or Feds to do a full-fledged report on the travelling habits of people to the island."

"Yeah," said Jack. "He was perplexed when he saw very few Chinese looking people getting off the boats, but saw a whole bunch of them getting on the boats for the ride to the mainland."

"A real racist," said Corbin. "How in the hell could he tell who was Chinese and who wasn't?"

"And then he stuck his nose in places that it didn't belong," said Jack.

"The bastard," said Corbin and took a slow drink.

"Started asking questions all around town," continued Jack. "Surveying the business owners on how many Chinese tourists they served per week, per month, and per year..."

"And then he got stupid," said Corbin.

"...And followed one of our groups onto the ferry and started asking *them* questions. Where did they come from, how did they get to Catalina. Like he was the damned FBI for crying out loud. Once they get on that ferry they're no longer our responsibility. There's someone hidden in the crowd who takes over, guides them to their next destination. We don't know who they are, and we don't want to know."

"The Chinese mafia, the Triad," said Corbin. "Must have latched onto that guy pretty quick."

"He disappeared," said Don. "The ferry had a record of him getting on the boat, he bought a round trip ticket, and he never came back. The Inn called our office a couple of weeks later to let us know that his room was abandoned, and they had to gather up his belongings and turn it all over to us. His family came over to pick it up, they put out a reward for information on his whereabouts. Last I heard he's still missing. It's been two years."

"Poor bastard," said Corbin and got up to get another beer. "Maybe they'll find him someday, what do you think?"

"Sure, and maybe they'll find the two retirees out of Newport who fell off their boat two years ago."

The group fell silent. Two years ago they lost another package under different circumstances, and since it wasn't their fault they didn't get involved. The guy missed his step getting off the cargo ship into the life raft and got swept under the giant ship with the stern wash. The retired couple was out for a cruise a couple of days later and found him, then started doing their own investigation and the Triad stepped in quickly.

Jack pointed his finger at Corbin. "Don't ever mess with them, you understand?"

Corbin's eyes narrowed and he spoke very slowly. "Don't you ever point your finger at me, and don't ever tell me what to do. No one can touch me on this island, no one, do you understand?"

"He's trying to help you," said Don. "You have a habit of throwing your weight around, and it might get you in trouble someday."

"When's our next shipment?" asked Kyle. "I need to get the boat ready."

"I don't know," said Jack. "Just get it ready."

11.

Jack got back to his house at exactly nine o'clock the next morning.

The ferry ride from Catalina was smooth as silk down-wind and down-swell and only took two hours.

He was still worried about Corbin, and his hot temper. Someday he'd do something stupid and get himself killed, Jack just hoped he wasn't anywhere nearby when it happened. They all knew about the married women and gambling debts and it was only a matter of time before someone put a bullet or two in him.

He pulled into the driveway and pushed the garage door opener on the dash.

Nothing.

He pushed it again and again and got no response from the door.

The little red light on the remote was flashing on when he pushed the button, but still nothing. Maybe it wasn't getting enough power, so he took the plastic back off and rotated the batteries, spun them in their bays, and tried again. Zero.

So he put the truck in park and got out, he'd have to do it the old fashioned way from inside the garage, and since he was out on the driveway, might as well check the mailbox.

He stepped towards the box and cursed when he saw the brown shape.

Damned little mutt up the street left him a deposit by the pole, and he narrowed his eyes and looked towards the old lady's house. He'd check the security footage to confirm, but he was sure it was her. Just because he'd kicked at the dog one time, she made a habit of bringing the mangy mutt here to do its business. So far there was nothing he could do about it. He didn't have clear footage that would prove that it was her, but maybe this time, lady, maybe this time.

He walked in the front door, tried a few light switches and shrugged his shoulders, realizing that the power was indeed off. He set the briefcase on the floor and instantly saw the broken window in the living room, a hole the size of a fist.

"Well, well what do we have here?" He whispered. He pulled a handgun from the holster at his back and moved cautiously into the house, checking each room, fully ready to blast a hole in anyone he saw. Finally convinced that whoever was stupid enough to break his window and break into his house was long gone, he relaxed and re-holstered the gun.

He looked closely at the window. One of the panes of the French window was busted completely out, and the shards were on the inside of the house below the window, but the latch was closed and locked. Maybe the culprit did not break into the house and just broke the window. Maybe a bird flew into the window.

There was one way to find out.

He went up the stairs to the office, flipped the switch on the battery back-up and turned on the computer, and clicked onto the security camera icon. He had three security cameras set up around the house, one at the front of the garage set next to the light, one in a clock on the wall in the living room, and one right here in the office. All of them battery powered for just the scenario that occurred.

He toggled through the living room footage first and sure enough, there was a fist going through the window, and then a shape going up and into the room. It looked like a man but there was no light and it was hard to make it out. The figure was carrying a red beamed flashlight.

Very smart. And then it got real close to the camera and he cursed. The guy was wearing a tight-fitting hoodie that covered his face, and tinted glasses that hid his eyes.

Bastard.

Then he toggled onto the office icon and shuffled the footage backwards till he saw the intruder right here where he was sitting.

He watched as the guy looked in the drawers but did not take anything, and he looked carefully at all the pictures on the wall, and how he paid close attention to the old picture when he was in China so many years ago. Then the intruder looked at his watch and hurried out of the room, out the window the way he came, and reached into the window to re-latch the lock.

Jack timed the footage from beginning to end, and noted that the intruder took nothing. From the time he entered the window, to the time he left was just about three minutes.

It wasn't a burglary. It was a reconnaissance mission.

12.

The office on the top floor of the building in the middle of Chinatown was anything but ornate. Five hundred square feet with high ceilings, light bamboo flooring, and green walls.

There was a large rectangular desk, three identical high backed chairs (one behind the desk and two facing it), a two-person wooden couch along one of the walls, a clock on the wall and a small good luck bamboo desk piece.

The middle-aged oriental man sitting in the chair behind the desk liked to have the world around him simple and clean, and to him simple and clean was elegance and wealth.

The man looked at his smart phone on the table, which was ringing, and noticed that the caller ID showed an area code of 310. Catalina Island. But he didn't recognize the other numbers. He picked up the phone and politely answered. "Yes."

The voice on the other end was abrupt and angry, the edges of the words slurred and mumbled, the man was drunk. "This Chang?"

"Who is this please?" he asked, still with a polite tone of voice.

"Listen up you piece of garbage slant eyed whore. You owe us twenty-five grand, and you are going to pay up, or we're coming after you. Understand?"

He waited for the man on the other end to finish. "I don't know what you are talking about."

"You know what I'm talking about you walking piece of horse dung with legs. Twenty-five grand. You try to rip us off, I'll come over there and tear you apart with my bare hands. Piece by piece. You don't know who you're dealing with here. Twenty-five. You got that? You pay up or I'm taking it out of your hide."

Again he was polite. "I mean I don't understand what you are talking about sir, because my name is not Chang. It is Smith. I believe you have the wrong number, goodbye."

He tapped on the red button on the face of the phone to end the call and sat there looking out the window at the wall of city buildings, stacked haphazardly to the horizon. The city surrounding his oasis was un-simple and un-clean.

The phone rang again, with the same caller ID as before. He let it ring until it went to voicemail which was a generic robot voice asking the caller to leave a message. After a while it rang again, from the same ID, and he let it go to voicemail again. And then the phone was silent. The small icon on the bottom right side of his phone now showed that he had two new voicemails, which he would listen to later.

For now though, the perfect afternoon schedule that he was used to enjoying was ruined. His cup of green tea to end the day, the evening jog through the park, an hour of martial arts and an hour of Tai Chi would have to wait.

He knew what happened. Jack was careless with his phone. Being careless could get you killed.

He tapped on his cell phone and dialed a number, which was answered right away. "Please come to my office," he said and hung up.

Five minutes later a young man knocked at the open door and entered. He was impeccably dressed in a grey suit with a light blue tie. He bowed to the man seated at the table and sat across from him.

The older man wasted no time. "I just received a call from one of our friends on Catalina. I don't know exactly how he got my number but that is beside the point. I think it's about time that I reconsider your proposal regarding that particular entry point for our product into the United States."

The other man nodded but kept silent while he listened.

"We've had a fairly good relationship with the Cabal, as they like to call themselves. Our goods have, with the exception of last week, always arrived on time. We have delivered on our promises to our people in China, which has made for a good and untroublesome business." He tapped his fingers together and leaned back in the chair. "Now however, their team is coming apart at the seams. I can sense that they will be a problem in the future, and have become a risk that we do not want to continue with."

"We're ready to take over," said the young man. "Whenever you give us the word."

"The profit from the human smuggling has been good. Two hundred and fifty thousand dollars per load, ten loads per year, two point five million per year. In five years we have made nearly thirteen million dollars. The technique that we have perfected is unmatched and nearly foolproof. However, it's unfortunate that the chief of police has prevented us from including drugs in our shipments. Our two and a half million per year could be ten million per year, fifty million over five years. It is time to streamline the operation and eliminate the middle man, so to speak."

The young man nodded. This is what he has been advocating for and he will finally get his way, but he holds his emotions in check, his face remains stoic, and he does not show an inkling of a smile, although that is what he is feeling inside. Finally the old man is listening to sense, and it apparently has been triggered by a phone call from someone in the Cabal. Perfect.

The old man continued. "If we could

arrange for the chief of police to have an unfortunate accident that couldn't be tied to us, like a fall off a cliff or getting run over by a car, then perhaps we could still utilize the rest of their team and the technique that they have developed to incorporate highly valuable drugs with our shipments. However, it appears that they now have a loose cannon in their midst. And he might not be the only one. Have your team mobilize and eliminate all four of the Cabal at one time."

"Yes Uncle."

"We'll instruct them that we have a shipment scheduled for in two days and you can use that opportunity for the hit. We won't actually have a shipment en route but they won't know that and they'll proceed as normal. We've observed their method of preparation. It's the same every time. They'll all be on their vessel at one time near midnight as they're getting ready for the pick-up at sea. It will be the perfect time to eliminate them all. Send two of our best assassins to Avalon two days ahead of time to scout out the location. They'll need to time it just right."

"Yes Uncle."

"That is all for now."

As Chang watched his assistant leave the room, he thought about Jack. He gave him plenty of time to remedy the situation, and bring his group together to include drugs in the shipments. As he told Jack on the park bench yesterday, everything is replaceable. He had his chance, and he failed.

13.

The two oriental men arrived on the four-thirty afternoon ferry to Avalon. No one would assume they were Chinese hit men from the cartel, here to complete a job.

He was impeccably dressed in brand new crisp golf attire, bright shirts and black slacks neatly pressed, and if you looked close enough you would notice that even their socks and golf hats had been hand pressed. New black shoes with a mirror shine.

They purposely looked and dressed like rich dorks.

They were pale and slim of build, spoke fluent Japanese to each other, and bowed quick and often. With their slick black hair, metal rimmed sunglasses and polite attitude, everyone assumed they were Japanese tourists on a sightseeing tour.

In fact, they were not one hundred percent Chinese, each had at least one quarter percent Japanese ancestry running in their veins due to the brutal Imperial Japanese Army occupation in world war two. In many ways that fact was a detriment to their development physically, spiritually and politically. Deep resentment within the general population still flowed and bubbled from the occupation and for good reason. Twenty-five million civilian and military Chinese lost their lives in the war that lasted eight years until the Japanese army surrendered on September 9, 1945.

They were at a disadvantage from the start and had to excel at everything they did just to stay even with the pack.

Raised in military families and members of the Red Army in their youth, they were now members of a different kind of army. The Chinese Triad. Highly trained in hand-to-hand combat, espionage, and every type of weapon and firearm that was ever made. If they came across a front loading ball and powder flint trigger rifle from the seventeenth century, they could make it work and take out the enemy.

They were excellent shots with modern sniper rifles, and each suitcase held the latest model with a breakdown barrel and metal stock, with both daytime and night-vision scopes.

Each of the assassins were fluent in their native Mandarin Chinese, and also in Japanese, English and Russian, with a working ability in the Germanic and Latin tongues. They could be sent anywhere on assignment by the Triad, go anywhere in the world, and blend in as tourists while understanding what was being said around and about them.

They disembarked from the ferry, bowing deeply to the purser on deck and thanking him profusely in a mix of Japanese and broken English. Each of them carrying their own small metal suitcase, they hailed one of the taxi's for a short ride up the hill to the hotel and checked into two adjoining rooms on the second floor facing the water.

Mr. Kubota and Mr. Saiki. Their ID's showing that they were from Tokyo. and The clerk smiled when he saw this and tried to speak Japanese.

"Doi to mustache," he said beaming. "I took Japanese in high school."

They smiled and bowed.

"Aw velly good, sank you," said the shorter man, and he pulled out a pocket book translator and flipped through the pages.

"Where best restaurant?"

The clerk smiled. "Well, you can't beat The Bent Whistle. It's two blocks over and they have the best buffalo steak this side of the Mississippi."

"Hai, Bent Whistle," the shorter man repeated and bowed as he took the electronic card keys, handed one to his friend, and headed for the elevator.

When they were settled in, front doors locked and double bolted, drapes across the windows, they opened the door between the rooms. They set their cases on one of the twin beds and checked their equipment.

One of the suitcases held what looked like a small hand-held radio with antenna sticking out of the top, but was in fact a device to check for electronic eavesdropping microphones and tiny cameras. It would detect the electronic transmission signal whether wireless or hard wired, whichever way it was connected. The taller of the two men walked around both rooms, sweeping it slowly and methodically in every crevice and corner, walls, floors, ceilings, over and under the beds, dressers, lights, around the TV and phones and windows, and all throughout the bathrooms. Every inch.

The other man put a piece of black tape across the peep hole on each of the front doors. He put a rolled up towel on the floor by the door where there was a gap, so no one could slide a mirror or small camera under the door.

They were taking no chances. This was standard operating procedure whenever they were staying at a hotel room, whether they were on a mission or not. It was common sense as far as they were concerned.

Finally satisfied that they were secure from prying eyes and ears, they checked the weapons first, assembled them quickly and maneuvered the triggers and firing pins.

They worked without talking, and when they were both convinced that the rifles were in the same perfect condition now as they were when they boarded the ferry in Long Beach, they each got out a daytime rifle scope and opened the drapes a crack on either side of the window that faced the harbor.

It was a scope, a telescope and a range finder. They each scanned the harbor and settled in on their target. The black catamaran moored in the middle.

Avalon had a simple mooring system. It was a round harbor like a giant open mouth and the moorings were strung in even, roundish lines from one side to the other, eleven in all. Each line contained additional mooring balls the closer you got to shore. The bigger boats were moored closer to the ocean and the smaller boats closer to the shore. You can cram a lot more little boats into the lines by the beach.

The black catamaran was moored in the third row from the entrance.

In some ways it was unfortunate that the mooring was in the middle, since at water level where they intended to set up their sniper positions, they might have to set their firing lines in between the other vessels that surrounded it. In other ways it worked to their favor since their target would be somewhat shielded from prying eyes on shore. From their earlier reconnaissance they knew that the boats moored immediately adjacent to and around the sailboat were mostly residents and were rarely used.

One of the sniper positions would be on the rock jetty at the entrance to the harbor on the northern side, while the other would be on the southern side creating a V shape firing pattern.

Four targets would be on the boat at the same time. Each of the assassins had two each as their marks, which they would eliminate within a split second of each other. Timing was critical. They would have wireless headsets to communicate with each other, and when all four targets were visible on deck with clear kill shot angles, a single word would begin the action and it would all be over before you could snap your fingers twice. Their rifles had noise suppressors on the barrel and subsonic rounds, which would greatly diminish the crack of the bullets firing. Plus, they would be down at water level on the rock jetties and the waves breaking and washing in the crevices would further mute the sound.

The only thing that they couldn't eliminate would be the muzzle flashes, but it would be over so fast that if someone thought they saw something, it would be too late to spot them on the rocks.

Two quick shots each and they would break down the rifles, pack them into the metal suitcases and be moving away from the area in less than half a minute.

The tall man nodded to the shorter one, who put on his sunglasses and went for a sightseeing walk down to the jetty to check out his sniper position, while his partner protected the equipment. He walked towards the end of the rock jetty, past the bars and restaurants, past the dock where the mainland ferries parked, and finally could go no further.

The jetty was fifteen feet above the water at a medium tide and was composed of rocks and boulders the size of small cars. Harvested from the east side of the island during the construction of the harbor at the turn of the century, they protected the interior of the harbor from surges and gave a foothold for the docks that housed the ferries.

He peered down at the apex of the jetty where the sea met the rocks. Someone was fishing down there, standing on a large flat rock casting a silver metal lure out into the harbor and retrieving it, reeling it in over and over. He made his way carefully down to investigate. It was a young teenage boy, blond-haired, tall and gangly, He greeted him with a wave, and a fake Japanese accent.

"Herow, pwenty fishes yes?"

The kid was startled and turned to look at him with fear and astonishment from the loud unexpected noise. Realizing that the funny man was just a tourist, he relaxed.

"Pwenty fish no," he replied dryly. "I've been here for over an hour and haven't had a single strike. This place sucks."

The man pointed at the water and made a motion with his hand held out flat and rising it.

"Maybe tide, yes?"

"Yeah maybe, I think the water's are just polluted here from those ferries over there." He pointed to the two ferries secured at their docks. "Why do you ask? Do you like to fish?" The funny tourist seemed keen on the water by the way he looked at it, plus his remark on the tide meant he had some kind of handle on the ocean.

The man lit up with a big smile and a loud voice. "Hai, I fish," and he pounded his chest and pointed at the rock that the teenager was standing on. "Tonight I fish here. Is okay?"

The kid laughed nervously. "It's fine with me dude. I don't think I'll ever try to fish at this spot again. In fact I'm done right now."

He reeled in the shiny lure, hooked it onto one of the eyes halfway down the pole, and picked up to his tackle box. He was getting creeped out by the funny looking tourist standing over him asking questions. "It's all yours dude." And he scrambled up the side of a rock and made his way up to the concrete walkway.

The man grinned sheepishly, pretending to be ignorant of what was being said, while his eyes were scanning the scene with military precision. He jumped down onto the now vacant rock and took it all in. He had a clear line of sight to the black catamaran from the flat rock, which was hidden from the top of the jetty. He could sit on the rock with his back to another rock for stability. The tide was medium at the moment and would be low at midnight so the rock would remain dry. Yes, this was perfect.

He stared at the catamaran which was pointed west into the prevailing wind sweeping into the harbor from the hills of the island. All the boats in the harbor were pointed east towards the wind. He was looking straight into the front of the catamaran, and could see directly into the wheelhouse. The winds were forecast to remain from the east through the night, so this was the view he would have. A clear line of fire as they were preparing to leave the harbor at midnight.

Right now the winds were in the ten knot range and if he were firing at this very moment he would calibrate his sight an eighth of a degree to the left to accommodate the wind against the bullet. When the time came and he was standing on the rock at midnight, he would calculate the wind speed and sight calibration.

It looked like it was exactly one hundred and fifty yards from the flat rock to the back of the boat, just like their estimate from the satellite maps. He would also use his rifle scope to get an exact range when the time came. There was no sense in bringing it with him now and drawing attention to himself.

He walked slowly back to the hotel observing every nook and cranny and cubby hole as he went. He stopped now and then, leaning over the handrail along the waterline and looked back towards the end of the jetty.

There were many places along the walkway where his flat rock was visible if you were looking directly at it. It would be midnight, cloudy with no moon, but the surrounding area would have dim lights, and the concern as always was the flash from the muzzle. Two shots, three at the most and he would be out of there. The only person who would recognize what it was would be someone who had been trained in firearms and had actually seen a muzzle flash at night. Otherwise from this distance it would look like someone was lighting a cigarette. Plus, they would have to be looking directly at the flat rock at the exact moment that he fired to see it.

Two quick shots, three at the most.

You worry too much, he told himself.

And that's why I'm here.

I take no chances, and the job gets done.

His mirrored sunglasses reflected the boats in the harbor. He paused in his thinking and reminded himself that the job gets done, every time no matter what may happen. This was his third hit in the past month, it had a strange feel to it. Most of his jobs were in the city, close up and personal. A window looking down onto a street, an alleyway, or a passing car stopped at a light and a bullet through the windshield.

A city where it was easy to escape with a car or a motorcycle. His last job, two weeks ago was at a villa on the outskirts of San Francisco.

Secluded in the hills, the villa had great perimeter security with one flaw: a line of trees two hundred yards away from the pool deck where his target was barbecuing a steak. They nearly got him after the hit but he managed to escape with the motorcycle through the hills and down into the maze of the city.

Here he was on an island and if something went wrong, the escaping part would be more difficult.

You worry too much, he told himself again. If something goes wrong you will never be caught. Alive that is. You will never be caught alive because that would be a thousand times worse that being caught dead. Your family would suffer greatly at the hands of the Triad. That's why he always carried a spare bullet.

For himself.

Two quick shots, three at the most.

He continued back to the hotel, walking slowly, studying the buildings as he went, cubby ways and escape routes, doors and windows and stairways leading up and out of danger, places to hide, places to run to and blend in, safety zones, from his rock on the edge of the harbor to the front door of the hotel, filing them all in the back of his mind for midnight.

Then, like a track athlete in a relay race handing the baton off to the next runner, the other shooter went on a stroll along the opposite side, the northern end of the harbor, past the Avalon Theatre to the long rock jetty and picked out his spot. He saw it with his own eyes: the exact rock where he would set up at midnight. He climbed down and stood on it, to feel it was solid with good grip.

Some tourists nearby were looking at him. He smiled at them and reached down to touch the water. Surprised at how cold it felt, he let out a little yelp. He was also a tourist, just passing by, testing the water of an unknown bay. The people looking at him shrugged their shoulders and went on their way. He continued with his preparation, observing his line of attack, and his target.

He also had a direct line of fire to the back of the catamaran, and since his angle was different from his partner, the wind off the hills coming directly into his face, he would most likely need no sight calibration.

Just like his partner, he walked slowly back to the hotel and studied the surrounding maze of escape routes.

There was the old Casino and the hillsides surrounding it, stairways leading up a away from the water, into the night. Nooks and crannies to hide and escape. As he made his way slowly back to the hotel, no one paid him the slightest attention. It was if he did not exist and blended into his surroundings.

14.

The reception area was pleasantly peaceful and quiet. Soft brown wall-to-wall carpet, dark wood paneled walls, gilded gold lamps with low wattage gentle lighting, and doors that closed with a whisper. All the colors were gentle and muted. But there was a slightly unpleasant smell: a background wisp of mothballs and embalming fluid.

The woman sitting at the desk in front of me in the mortuary was very pleasant in her unhelpfulness.

She looked like she was probably in her mid to early thirties, plump but not overweight, solid with a Slavic build for raising children or castle walls, long blond hair that looked like it was brushed a hundred times a day, and dimples on cheeks that deepened as she smiled, which seemed to be perpetual.

Since I'd entered the door and stood in front of her, she hadn't stopped smiling. For someone who dealt with dead people all the time she seemed unusually upbeat and cheery.

Maybe it was her way of offsetting the morbid situation of being in close proximity to the recently departed and the people who were left behind, or maybe it was just her natural good-hearted being.

Either way, it wasn't doing me any good. She smiled sweetly while shrugging her shoulders and with a sugary voice declared that there was nothing she could do for me.

"I'm sorry sir, but since you are *not* the next of kin I cannot divulge any information about the deceased."

"What if I told you I was her husband?"

She looked startled. "Are you?"

"No, but what if I was?"

"Well of course," she said flatly. "That would qualify as next of kin. That's the definition of next of kin. Of course you would need to provide proof such as a marriage certificate." Her sugary demeanor was souring.

"What if I told you I was her husband and even though you knew it wasn't true, you just looked the other way and gave me all the details I'm looking for."

All the expression drained out of her face. The joyful eyes turned blank, the smiling corners of her mouth turned downward. She was tired of playing my little game and no reply was forthcoming.

"So you can't tell me what the cause of death was?"

"No."

"I'm the one who found her you know."

"Yes sir, I know that now."

"Can you at least tell me if an autopsy was performed?"

She shook her head. Her lips pursed together tightly like she'd just taken a bite out of a bitter lemon, and she sighed heavily.

"Can you at least tell me if she's still here?"

"Yes, that I can tell you."

"And?"

"Yes, she is still here."

"Have any of her next of kin called or inquired?"

"Unfortunately, no."

"Have the police made any headway in their investigation? Do they have any leads?"

Her eyes narrowed and her smile was tinged with evil intent, for this was her golden chance to get me out of there. "Now why don't you ask them that question?" Her sugary voice was out of place with her facial expression.

I was done pestering the poor lady. I found the woman and brought her to shore, but I couldn't get the smallest bit of info out of an undertaker's wife. I would fail miserably as a detective.

She shuffled some papers on her desk and looked back up, seemingly surprised that I was still there and raised her eyebrows in dismissal. "Now if you don't mind, I have a lot of work to do."

Sure you do lady.

I walked out of the mortuary and headed down the street towards the police station in the middle of town. Maybe they found out the same thing I did, that the girl didn't even live at the address on her driver's license.

I decided to have a drink in a bar and think for a little while. Sometimes when I needed to figure something out, I'd head to a noisy place with a lot of people, and the way I had to keep my attention focused on everyone around me it somehow had a way of increasing the blood flow to my brain, triggering my synapses or something. I don't know, it worked for me.

I liked the little bar that we sat in when we first got to the island with Cody and Tony Piper and so I headed over there. It had a nice view of the water and a good vibe.

I walked in the front door and headed to the exact table I'd sat in a few nights ago and settled into the exact chair as before, set against the stucco wall with a view of the harbor.

It was ten o'clock in the morning and the sun was shining at an angle that made the water look grey. I could see the Spice tucked in between a thirty-five-foot ketch and a forty-foot power boat, but the black catamaran was nowhere in sight.

Must be out on a pirate sailing adventure, I thought. When I was walking through town I saw a few hand-outs advertising the three-hour pirate cove snorkel and lunch tour.

There was a waitress taking an order at a table across the room, and a bartender making bloody Mary's for three people sitting at the bar and talking loudly, twenty tables in the bar, and five had customers, including myself. It was a slow morning.

At one of the tables near the entrance sat a fairly beautiful brunette who was fiddling with a straw in a tall glass of iced tea, just stirring and stirring, and watching me.

She looked to be in her late twenties, early thirties at the most. I nodded to her when I entered the bar. She was sitting in the shadow so as my eyes got used to the difference in lighting it was hard to see what I was looking at when I passed her. Now as I watched her over there watching me I realized just how stunning she was.

Super beautiful women can be unnerving to the uninitiated, they sensed a power over the opposite sex who they could turn weak at a single glance. Sometimes the vicious ones used it for sport, and she was approaching that level.

She had the kind of long luscious brown hair that naturally curved very slightly throughout its length and settled on her tan and bare shoulders just right.

Large gold hooped earrings with diamonds on the ends that sparkled in the morning sun and said 'look at me' framed her face. She was wearing a low cut peasant blouse that ran straight across the tops of her ample breasts, and her eyes were bright and inquisitive, sort of wild in nature with long suggestive eyelashes, while her mouth was full lipped, pouty, and bored.

Never one to back off a challenge such as this, I returned her gaze without flinching, and nodded to her again.

Her pouty bored mouth bent over and took a long sip of her drink without taking her eyes off me, staring at me for close to a minute to see if I'd flinch, and seeing that I wasn't going to back down, she rose gently from her chair and walked towards my table to stand in front of me, blocking my view of the water with her curves.

Somehow I didn't mind.

"Can I get you a drink?" She asked.

"Are you a waitress?"

She smiled at that. "You're pretty sure of yourself aren't you?"

"I didn't mean to be."

"Did you come over on the ferry?"

"I have my own ride."

"That's what I thought."

"Explain."

"You see those three tourists sitting at the bar drinking bloody Mary's at ten o'clock in the morning?"

"You mean the ones who were trying to get your attention when I came in?"

"They came over on the ferry."

"How can you tell?"

"You see how boisterous they are? How loud, and show-offish? They're pretenders, here for the day or the night, but pretenders nonetheless. They might be able to afford a boat, but they couldn't navigate it across a bathtub."

"You're pretty good at this."

"I live here, I see it every day. Sometimes it offends me and I have to get as far away as possible from here, and other times when I see someone on the island who's self-confident, calm and assured, that makes me happy. Very happy in fact."

I glanced down at her hands that held the iced tea, and she gently sighed, and held up her left hand with the large diamond encrusted wedding ring.

"Oh yeah, by the way, I'm married."

The offhand way she said it and the look on her face didn't make it sound too thrilling.

"Happens to the best of them," I shrugged.

"I see it hasn't happened to you." And she nodded towards my hands. No ring.

"People that are married don't always wear a ring."

"So are you?"

"Does it matter?"

She smiled at that and her face got soft and dreamy, trying to make the best bedroom eyes that she could manage. Of course it didn't matter, not to her.

"I own this bar," she said. "Or, should I say my husband and I own this bar." She hesitated, sizing me up one last time, looking at my eyes, and then bent down and whispered near my ear. "But he doesn't own me." Her breath with a hint of vodka was warm against my earlobe, and her perfume lingered in my nostrils as she stood straight again, and she smiled, empowered at her statement of independence. "So I ask again, can I get you a drink?"

"Club soda over ice with a big wedge of lime,

or two if they're cut small."

In my line of work I'd come across a few vicious cold blooded killers, and none of them held a candle to this broad. This woman was dangerous. I'm sure Amber would have some different words to describe her, maybe a short sentence that ended with slut. And as I watched her swish her tail for my benefit towards the bar I felt sorry for her schmuck of a husband, whoever the poor bastard was.

The last time I flirted with a dame in a bar, her boyfriend shot me in the ass from across a loading dock and I nearly bled to death.

This broad was married and there was no telling what could happen to me if she tried to get cozy. I decided to keep it cool. I was just playing around and didn't think it was going to go this far. She called my bluff and whispered in my ear. All I wanted now was to pay for my drink, take a couple of sips and get the hell out of there in one piece.

When she returned with the drink, I pulled out my wallet and set it on the table.

"How much do I owe you?"

"The drinks on the house," she purred.

"I insist," I said as I pulled out a five dollar bill.

"No I insist," she said and put her hand on my mine.

I slowly pulled my hand back so as not to offend her. "Look," I said. "I'm really flattered and all, you're very beautiful, but I'm not interested."

That seemed to amuse her and she smiled

and tapped her toe and tilted her head.

"Why, are you gay?"

The question was a challenge, and it showed that she had a mean streak. Obviously this woman was so incredibly gorgeous and had gotten her way with men for most of her adult life, that to her, the only ones able to resist her charms must not be attracted to women at all.

"The truth is, that I could never, ever, and I repeat ever fool around with..." I let the sentence dangle for a moment, "...a brunette. I really only like blondes," I lied. "Sorry, it's just one of those things."

She narrowed her eyes and shook her head. "Bullshit." She didn't like my little joke and now she was getting pissed off, I could see the anger building in the corners of her eyes.

"Okay you caught me," I said. "Truth is I'm engaged to be married to a wonderful girl. She's the love of my life, my soul-mate." I shrugged my shoulders and smiled. "What can I say, I'm toast."

She studied me for a moment to see if I was telling the truth this time.

"Now that's more believable." She tried to salvage some of her pride and with a whip of her head threw her hair over her shoulder. "So what makes you think I was coming onto you anyways? I told you I was married."

She reached down and sullenly picked up the five dollar bill.

"It's three fifty for the soda water with lime. I'll bring your change."

"Keep the change," I said, and tried to give

144

her back some of her lost honor. "And by the way I'm sorry for thinking you were coming onto me, you're just so damned beautiful I thought that I was day-dreaming."

I winked at her. I could see that she was torn between a smile and a frown. She settled on the frown and walked away without the extra shimmy this time.

15.

The Avalon Sheriff's station is located one block from the harbor on Sumner Avenue.

Sitting in his air-conditioned office on the ground floor, the Watch Commander, Sergeant Don Baker's attention was consumed by the stack of paper on his desk.

The big cheese, the Station Commander was still on the mainland and every request for manpower, supplies, and equipment went through him. Which meant that Don would need to wade through the pile. He shook his head and made a command decision. All official business would have to wait for a couple of hours. He pushed that stack to the side, and brought another stack to the center. Personal business first. He measured the stack with his two fingers, about five inches tall, he surmised. Credit card bills and business statements, daily ledger reports. Half a million dollars a year from his little smuggling operation wasn't a huge amount of money, but it took some effort to wash it, put it through the laundry so it was legit as far as the bean counters at the federal and state tax offices were concerned. Add to that the Police ethics and integrity department, which was geared towards investigating any potential graft in the department: bribes, kickbacks, extortion, all the bad things a cop could use to get extra cash under his belt, and he had to be careful.

Spending the half million per year wasn't the hard part, just ask his wife and take a look at the stack of receipts in front of him. She was on a yearlong party, from New Year's day to New Year's Eve. Every other week it seemed, she was off to the mainland to see her sick mother, or help a friend with an event, and while she was there a lot of shopping needed to be done.

Sometimes she needed to get farther away and went with her girlfriends to Tahiti, or Maui. Still, it wasn't too bad most of the time. He knew that he married way over his head, cheerleader at Long Beach High, prom Queen, it went on and on. She was a genuine beauty, and he was lucky to snag her away from all the other bastards who were trying to hook up with her. It took every bit of conniving and money and energy he had in the beginning to keep her attention on him, and him alone. And now it was nearly half a million a year.

He separated the stacks of paper into three smaller stacks. Receipts from personal credit card purchases, cash receipts from the bar, and receipts for supplies for the bar. It was actually pretty easy. Half a million dollars divided by three hundred and sixty-five was a measly thirteen hundred and change per day. The bar was doing pretty good, averaging three grand in receipts per day, so he just added thirteen hundred in cash sales every day to the till, and voila. Take out the cost of the food, booze, cooks, bartenders, insurance, lease rent, utilities, and after paying the state and federal tax on what remained, he cleared a tidy four hundred grand per year, plus his sheriff's pay of fifty grand. You could live pretty large on that amount of money, and as far as the government was concerned, he was legit.

16.

It was a ten minute walk from the bar to the Harry L. Hufford Government Complex which housed the Sheriff station, courthouse, library and county offices down a street lined with shops and restaurants, and parked up and down that street were dozens of golf carts with the odd car here and there. Ironically, a Chinese restaurant specializing in Mandarin Cuisine was two doors down from the little civic center.

"Can I help you?" The uniform standing behind the plexiglass window was pleasant and straight to the point.

"I'd like to talk to the Station Commander."

"He's not in. Is there something I can help you with?"

"When's he coming back?"

"Wednesday. Can it wait?"

I shook my head. "Is there someone filling in for him?"

"Sergeant Baker is the Watch Commander. He's in his office. Can I ask what this is about?"

"I'm the guy who found the body in the ocean on Saturday. I just want to see how the investigation is going."

He nodded. "Okay, what's your name."

"Badger Thompson."

He gave me that look that everyone did when they heard my name.

"You mean like the animal?"

I just nodded and he didn't press the issue.

"Okay, just sign this form, let me see your ID and we'll get you in."

He passed a clipboard under the opening in the window and I printed and signed my name, put my driver's license on the clipboard and slid it back under the window. He took a quick look then returned the license and opened the door to the side. I followed him in through the office.

He knocked and then opened the door to the small office down the hallway. The sergeant looked up from his pile of paperwork.

"Yes?"

"This is Badger Thompson to see you sir. He's the guy who found the body in the ocean on Saturday."

I could see by his eyes he was startled, and then calmed himself.

"Sure, come on in. Have a seat." He stood up without making a comment about my name, and motioned to the two chairs in front of his desk. The officer left the room and closed the door. I reached over and shook the deputy's hand and he introduced himself.

"Don Baker, how can I help you?"

I didn't say anything at first as I sat in the chair on the right side. My eyes scanned the office, the neat and tidy framed citations, awards, certifications, photos on the walls. My gaze lingered a little longer on one particular photo and he followed my eyes to see which one it was. A wedding picture, a younger version of the man who was sitting in front of me right now, standing stiff and starched in a tuxedo, holding his hat in one hand, and the hand of his blushing bride in the other, dressed in a flowing white wedding dress, with long black hair and wild eyes.

The girl from the bar.

He noticed my attention on the picture. "My wife Amanda."

I nodded and looked directly at him, so this was the poor bastard who was married to the man eater.

"I met her at your bar just before I walked over here."

His eyes narrowed nearly imperceptibly with suspicion, but I saw it. The jealous husband.

"She introduced herself as the owner," I continued. "I was there a couple of days ago, on a Friday, and thought it had a pretty good view of the harbor, so I thought I'd go back and have a soda. Friday night was hopping, we were lucky to get a table, but it's slow in there today, not much happening."

"Crowds come and go, with the weekend. As predictable as the tide."

I got to the point. "We were here in Avalon

Friday night and Saturday morning. We were here for the party at the Zane Grey estate."

"And?"

"Saturday morning we took a sail along the north coast, and found the body of the woman, and turned it over to the Coast Guard. I'm just curious how the investigation is going, and if anyone has come forward to claim the body. I was at the mortuary earlier this morning, they couldn't help me." I motioned to the pile of papers in front of him. "Sorry, I can see you're busy."

He nodded, dug under another pile, and pulled out a thin manila folder. He looked through it, then read a paragraph.

"On November Twenty-First at eleven hundred hours, Badger Thompson, captain of the forty-five foot sailboat the "Sugar" found the body of a female approximately thirty-five years of age one half mile outside of Arrow Point, Catalina Island." He looked up from the folder. "Do you have identification?"

I nodded.

He held out his hand. "Can I see it?"

I pulled out my wallet and handed him my California driver's license. He looked it over carefully front and back, then pulled out a small flashlight from the top drawer of his desk, shined a small blue light on it. I knew that it was an ultraviolet flashlight, a black-light that every bar door bouncer and airport TSA agent carried to spot fake ID's. I decided to play dumb.

"What's with the light?"

"Embedded water mark, the black light makes it visible. Old habit. You're legit." He still held the card and looked closer at the front. "Your address is a boat slip in Dana Point Harbor."

Again I just nodded. "It's a place to hang my hat."

He handed me back the card. "It's a hell of a thing to find a dead body anywhere. But out in the ocean..." His voice trailed off and he shook his head and frowned.

"It wasn't very pleasant." I was thinking that I sure wish I'd had that ultraviolet black light to shine on Mei Ling's driver's license the day we found her. I needed to get my hands on one.

"Did you sail back over in the Sugar today?"

I studied him, but unlike the deputy my eyes did not narrow even though my suspicions had been aroused. I hadn't told him that I left the island after the finding the body, so why would he assume that I had sailed back over today?

"I had a problem with the Sugar, so I left it in Dana Point and brought my other boat over."

The inflection of his voice rose a notch and he said it more as a statement than a question. "You have two boats?" I could see he was surprised.

I shrugged my shoulders. "It's good to have a back-up. Anyways, the girl was carrying a large amount of money, and a driver's license with a Long Beach address."

He flipped through some pages in the file and nodded. "Yes, that's true."

"How much did it count out to? I was estimating about ten grand. Was I right?"

"I can't give out that information."

"What about the address on the license? Did someone go and check it out?"

"I'm sure someone did, we forwarded this file to the LAPD to follow up on it."

"Any response yet?"

He closed the file and sighed. "Well, Mr. Thompson this is an open investigation and as such I really can't give you any details. I hope you understand."

I did not understand. I was being stonewalled and I didn't like it.

He leaned forward, and gave me his tough guy look. "But since I have you sitting in front of me, perhaps I can ask why you're so curious?"

The way he asked the question made it sound like he thought I was a suspect. What he didn't know is that it would take someone a lot tougher than him to make me crack and walk away.

"I don't like mysteries. They keep me up at night. I found the body, and as such I think I have the right to make sure the family of this person knows what happened to her."

"Do you have any idea how many deceased bodies went unclaimed in Los Angeles County just last year?"

I shook my head.

He reached behind his chair to a bookcase and pulled out a binder and opened it up to a page near the front and put his finger in the middle of it and read off the numbers.

"One thousand five hundred and fifty."

"C'mon," I snorted. "That seems pretty high. Fifteen hundred unidentified bodies? You got to be kidding me."

He shook his head. "I'm not talking unidentified, I'm talking unclaimed. They die at home, hospitals, homeless shelters, and on the streets. Funerals are expensive, times are tough and sometimes it's easier for the family to just look the other way and let the State take care of it."

"Alright well how many of those were classified as unidentified?"

He looked back at the page with his finger on it. "Unidentified, and those that were unidentifiable totaled eleven. Four men, three women, and four whose gender was unknown."

"How many on Catalina?"

"None."

"What about the body I found?"

"She's unclaimed, not unidentified."

"Getting back to those fifteen hundred not unidentified, but unclaimed deceased bodies, they must have had ID's then. Right? You know who they are, or who they were since they had some type of identification."

"Sure."

"How many of those had fake ID's? Did someone shine the black light and see the embedded water mark on all those ID's? It would seem that would be company policy for identifying dead people to make sure they had the right person."

His eyes glazed over and his face went blank. He was done with me, and yet he knew where this was headed.

"Bear with me," I said. "I'm just trying to figure this out, I'm new to this whole unclaimed body scene. Did anyone shine a black light on Mei Ling's ID?"

A tiny bead of sweat appeared in middle of his forehead.

He didn't say anything right away so I tried to help him out. "The dead girl at the mortuary."

"I know who you're talking about. I didn't personally shine the UV light on the ID that was found with her, and to tell you the truth I wish I had."

"We can go over there now and shine it."

"The only thing at the mortuary is the body."

"Do you still have the evidence?"

I wasn't going away. He nodded, resigned to the fact that the easiest way to get me out of his hair was to shine the light on the ID. He picked up the phone.

"Darnell, please bring me the evidence bag from the Mei Ling case."

It took about five minutes for a stocky brunette woman in her early forties to show up carrying a zippered blue bag which she handed to Don. She stood on the side and waited as he opened it and pulled out a double bagged wad of cash, and a double bagged driver's license and set them both on top of the desk in front of him. Then he reached behind his chair and pulled out a brand new pair of evidence handling gloves, slipped them on and opened the bags containing the license. He held it by the edges and studied it front and back, just the way he had for my ID. Then he picked up the black-light and shined it on the front, and shook his head and turned it so I could see.

"The ID looks completely legit, but there's no watermark," he said. "How did you know?"

"Just a hunch."

He carefully put the ID back in the double bags, then into the blue zippered bag.

We were all three looking at the bagged wad of money still sitting on the desk.

I said out loud what we were all thinking. "I wonder if the money is legit, or counterfeit?"

"It'll take more than a black light to determine that," said Don. "We'll send this over to our forensics department on the mainland to look it over, see what they can find out." Then he placed the money back in the blue bag and handed it to Darnell. "Send this with an armed guard on the next helicopter to Los Angeles." She nodded and left the room.

"Anything else?"

"The officer on the Coast Guard ship that rode with me after finding Mei Ling, told me that the same sort of thing happened a couple of years ago."

"I'd have to dig in the files. Doesn't ring a bell."

"A body doesn't ring a bell?"

"Maybe it wasn't found in our jurisdiction. Maybe they found a body and took it straight to Long Beach since it was closer, or they were on another mission in that area. I know it doesn't look like it, and we don't try to advertise it, but we're a pretty busy island. We average ten incidents a day, over three thousand per year, all types of crimes and what I like to call 'events', where people do stupid things and get themselves killed. Boating, scuba, hiking, fishing accidents. People leave the comfort of their homes and steady lives, come over to Catalina and do things that are out of their ability and pay the price. They get drunk, roll golf carts, crash boats, get lost in caves underwater, you name it, we have it."

He was lying. I could see it in his eyes.

"So what happens now," I asked. "It's been three days since I found her."

He nodded. "Official policy kicks in. If an un-identified body isn't claimed within seven days, the body is cremated and the ashes sent to the public cemetery."

"Mind if I stop back in once in a while to check in?"

He hesitated a split second then smiled to cover it. "Sure, come in anytime, you're always welcome."

17.

Corbin finished the last of his reps for the day, full squats with a one hundred pound free weight barbell in each hand, set tight against each of his shoulders as he squatted deep. As he reached a full standing position he brought the weights over his head and rotated them in a circle, wincing in pain as his arms and legs reached the threshold of exhaustion. He threw the barbells on the padded floor in front of his feet and they bounced with a clang towards the wall.

He took deep breaths and calmed his heart-rate. The large veins in his chest and legs were thumping.

His daily two-hour workout was complete. He settled his massive frame into a simple wooden chair near the front door and looked towards the harbor. The morning sun was glinting off the water and he could just about make out the mast of the Black Cat rising above the pile of boats. Kyle would be on board making sure it was sea-worthy for their trip to the shipping lane and a package pick-up. Damned if he was going to let a filthy Chinaman make him drop another package. I'll break them in half before I'll let another one get away, he thought.

Sweat streamed down his face, arms and legs. He shut and locked the door so he could go take a shower. He patted the barrel of the double-barreled shotgun propped next to the doorframe, and for good measure picked it up and checked the cartridge. It was loaded. He popped both cartridges out and back in with a snap. There was a shotgun at every doorframe in the house, and one under his bed. You could never be too careful.

He passed a mirror in the hall as he was heading to the bathroom and flexed his forearm. His jet black hair slicked back, face chiseled and square, six foot four, two hundred fifty pounds of tanned muscle, halfblooded Italian, halfblooded Spanish, full blooded home-wrecker.

The way he figured, it wasn't his fault if a husband couldn't control his wife. Half the time he never even knew the gal was married till afterwards. Women came in droves to Catalina to let their hair down and get wild. As soon as they saw him sitting at the bar they'd take off their rings, and hence the old saying, no rings, no strings.

He wasn't a cop after all. He couldn't run a background check on every woman who came onto him, so how was he supposed to know who was married and who wasn't if they wouldn't wear their ring for crying out loud?

Except for Don's wife, Amanda. She was most definitely married, in fact he'd been one of the grooms in the wedding party. And even then it wasn't his fault. She came onto him so strong that he had to finish the deal or someone else would have. After all, what are friends for?

She was in Vegas two years ago with her girlfriends from Long Beach High School on the very same weekend that he decided to fly into the desert city to get in some gambling and woman action. Ten ex-cheerleaders in sin city for a bachelorette party that was bound to spiral out of control. She was a little bit tipsy when she spotted him at the poker table and went right over and sat in his lap and started kissing his neck with her soft lips.

That night might have been the beginning of the end for her marriage, or she may have been up to the same stuff all along. She was one of the hottest women he'd ever seen even to this day, and friend or no friend he folded his cards with one hand, grabbed her with the other, took her up to his hotel room, and bedded her for the entire night and half the morning, until he got tired of her and threw her out the door.

Unfortunately, that seemed to turn her on even more and now she was pounding on his door all the time. She liked being turned down and thrown out and ignored, that type of behavior drove her crazy.

And it happened all the time. All types of women, engaged, with a boyfriend, married or not, throwing themselves at him. Hence the shotguns by the doors and under the bed.

He wiped the sweat off his chest, threw the towel on the ground and opened the cupboard by the hallway for a fresh one. What the hell, he muttered, "I thought there was one left..."

"Looking for something?" Came a small soft voice from the bedroom. He nearly jumped out of his skin. He glanced quickly around the corner with wide eyes, thinking he should grab his shotgun first, and there he saw his missing white fresh towel and nothing else wrapped around Amanda's tan glistening skin, as she lay on the bed, cradling her head with a cupped hand and looking at him with those eyes.

"How'd you get in here?"

"The side door. You left it unlocked."

Damn, he thought she sure looked good and at this point in time with the testosterone packed blood rushing through his body he was in no mood to argue about her breaking and entering his house.

She took off her earrings and laid them on the end table next to the bed.

"Do you want me to leave?" She asked.

He shook his head and moved towards the bed.

"Not yet."

18.

Kyle finished screwing the brand new stainless steel cleat into the rail of the deck of the Black Cat and checked his work.

"Solid," he pronounced after wrapping a rope through around the toggles, standing upright and tugging on it until he was red in the face. The old cleat had a hairline crack running down the middle of it and probably would have held for a few more months, but there was no sense gambling with it. Fifty bucks for the new cleat versus being out of business.

"Now for the fun part." He looked straight up at the top of the mast, the runner cleat at the apex needed replacing, eighty-five feet off the deck. Like climbing an eight-story building the width of a coffee can. When you got to the top it seemed like you were at the tip of an eighty-five foot pencil. "No problem," he muttered, and set up his one man climbing device: a modified mountain climbing rig with foot straps, carabiners, and belay device.

The whole boat was constructed of carbon fiber, including the mast which alone cost nearly a hundred thousand dollars. But it didn't stop there. Carbon fiber composites give off a radar signature, although much fainter than aluminum. The carbon fiber hull and mast of the Black Cat were also coated with a sandwich layer of Kevlar, which did not give off a radar signature. The stainless steel cable rigging that held the mast in place front back and sides were also wrapped with black Kevlar tape. During their very first semi-annual Coast Guard inspection, the new inspector asked Kyle about the Kevlar wrapping.

Bob was a nice enough guy on his last tour with the Guard before he retired. He wasn't out to make a name for himself, just trying to dot the i's and cross the t's before he sailed off to retired land, cashing government paychecks for the rest of his life.

"What's with the wrapping on the mast rigging?"

"I don't know," Kyle said with a shrug of his shoulders. "I heard it extends the life of the cable when you're on the ocean. Plus it looks cool, being black makes our boat look more badass, and the tourists love it."

That part was true, the tourists that came over on the ferry did love the all-black catamaran, with the black skull and crossbones flag on top of the mast. The trip around the corner of the island to Pirate Cove was a highlight, especially for the kids who got to wear pirate hats, shoot the water cannons on the deck, and pretend they were heading out to battle other pirate ships and find buried treasure on the beach.

"Why are you using Kevlar anyways? If I didn't know better I'd think you were trying to avoid radar detection." Bob laughed.

Kyle shook his head with an impatient frown. "What? Are you kidding? Why the hell would we want to do that? Man you guys are paranoid. It's a pretend pirate boat Bob, not a real one. We give pirate boat rides to kids and families from the mainland. Here, try on this hat, you get a free one with every ride, plus it's great advertising." Kyle reached into an iron black treasure chest on the deck and took out a brand new black pirate hat with a skull and cross bones on the front and handed it to Bob. Under the skull and crossbones was the name of their boat, 'The Black Cat'.

Bob also frowned. "Thanks, I'll give it to one of my kids. Now what about that wrapping?"

"From what I heard Kevlar is stronger than steel. I'm just doing what I'm told Bob."

Blaming his partners. It was always best to deflect blame from yourself to some nameless, faceless third party. "The investors said it's good for the rigging, so I'm wrapping it."

"Well, they don't know what the hell they're talking about, so you're going to have to unwrap it for every inspection so we can check the cables for wear and tear. If that rigging gets corroded undetected and snaps under stress, we're all gonna go in front of the firing squad. "

So twice a year Kyle unwrapped, and then re-wrapped the cables from top to bottom, it took about ten hours each time and was a real pain in the rear, climbing up and down the mast and hanging on the rigging. But it was worth it, and had made them millions.

Their boat was completely undetectable by radar and had gone un-noticed at night sailing into the shipping lane to pick up immigrants for four years now without a hitch. Four years, twice a month and nearly a hundred runs to the lane. Two hundred grand per run. Twenty million in cash, five million per man.

Kyle liked to think about money as he worked, add it up and multiply it, and when he looked at it that way, it wasn't such a pain un-wrapping and re-wrapping after all. And he even started humming a little tune as he hoisted himself up the mast.

Five million in cash, and he'd saved all of it. A million and a half in the bank, and the rest vacuum sealed in stainless steel canisters and buried in deep holes all around his property, at the house his Mom left him, God bless her heart.

The hell with investing and taking a chance on losing in a stock market crash, or letting a bank hold onto it. When he retired, if he wanted some extra cash, he'd just go in the back yard, dig up a few thousand, and cut the red tape.

He vaguely knew what the other guys did with their portion, but in the end it didn't really matter. In the very beginning they made a pact, do what you want with your share, but be smart, don't wave it around or get in trouble with the IRS. Hide the proceeds, wash it any way you could, just don't drag the other guys into trouble.

Jack bought a little house in Avalon that he converted into a real clubhouse with a pool table, and cinema center. He also bought a house in Long Beach where he spent most of his time, with his motorcycle buddies.

Corbin inherited his Dad's house on the hill overlooking the harbor, drinking and womanizing and gambling away just about every penny he made.

Don married the girl of his dreams, the super-hot Amanda who spent every dime that he made and was turning his hair prematurely grey with her antics. Rumors swirled around that girl, and Kyle actually felt a little sorry for Don.

Kyle had no drama, or problems and led a fairly stable life. His job was taking care of the boat, making sure it was in top shape for their trips out to the lane, and running it like a legitimate business, which in fact it was, part-time.

He took on the burden of endless maintenance, supplies, equipment, licensing, dock fees, insurance, employees, and as a bonus got to keep all the proceeds.

They ran a two-hour expedition to Pirate Cove twice a day, every day. They supplied the food, beer, snorkel gear, and hats, and packed them in twenty at a time for fifty bucks a head, two grand in gross receipts per day. He had five crewmen and women rotating in and out and he personally captained every trip. After all expenses, he netted a little over a grand per day, which came out to around four hundred grand extra per year. Add that to the smuggling money and he was netting close to a million every year.

It seemed like yesterday, but it was ten years ago that Jack got out of the Army and came home. His last stint was an assistant Army liaison at the US Embassy in Beijing. It was there that he met some interesting people who were starting a new business and needing partners in America.

Jack gathered his three friends at their ramshackle clubhouse on the outskirts Avalon. At the time their clubhouse consisted of a couple of sheets of discarded construction plywood and two-by-fours, with a mud floor and rocks to sit on that they'd made when they were in grade school, secretly tucked into a patch of scrub brush beneath Wrigley Road looking out over the harbor. Jack pulled out a twelve-pack of beer, handed one to each of them and made a proposal.

It started like this:

"How would you all like to be filthy rich?"

It wasn't a tough sell, since they were all dirt poor at the time, just scraping by with odd jobs. Corbin selling jewelry to the tourists by the pier, Don working security at a nearby hotel and trying to get on the police force, Kyle renting snorkel gear at a little corner store.

And Jack, newly retired from the Army but without enough years for a pension.

Jack laid out the plan that he'd ironed out with his friends from China.

"The cargo ships are going to slow down just enough to drop off a small lifeboat with ten immigrants a few miles north of Catalina. We rendezvous with a separate vessel and the immigrants board our boat. We scuttle the lifeboat to get rid of the evidence, and we take them to Catalina and put them on the ferry the next day. We get ten grand per person, that's a hundred grand per trip."

Don was the first one to agree, before Jack even finished with his pitch. As soon as he heard the words 'hundred grand' he was on the team. "I'm in," he said.

He was pioneering a girl he met from Long Beach, a real hot tomato, fresh out of high school, and was spending every dime he had to wine and dine and impress the girl, but his little piddly security pay it wasn't enough to keep her full attention, and there were other suitors trying to wedge their way in. He was in danger of losing her at any minute.

"You know it's against the law to smuggle people, right?" Asked Jack. "Aren't you trying to get on the police force?"

"I don't care," said Don. He was desperate.

"I just want to make sure you know what you're getting into. We're all friends and if you feel like it's going to get in the way of your new career, then just walk right out of here, and don't bother with us, and we won't bother with you."

"I'm in I tell you, and don't try to talk me out of it." His face was grim. "By next month I'll be on the force. I'll have a guaranteed job here on Catalina, and I'll be on the inside."

With a little bit of money that Jack had saved, and some seed money from the Triad, they rented a small fishing boat and did a trial run to the lane. They picked up a handful of sad and seasick Chinese on a moonless night in the middle of the summer. Brought them back to Avalon, scrubbed them, clothed them and sent them on their way on the ferry to Long Beach the next morning. It netted them a hundred thousand dollars, twenty five grand each, and they were on their way.

Two more runs in the rented boat and a close call with the Coast Guard told them they needed to make some quick adjustments.

Coming back from the lane two hours after midnight with ten seasick and scared Chinese stashed in the cramped front hull, they were overtaken by the cutter and hailed by the officer on deck as the boat pulled alongside. The officer shined the searchlight into their little vessel.

There is no Fourth Amendment when it comes to a boat on the waterways of the United States, and the Coast Guard can board and search any vessel at any time of day or night, whether docked or moored, in rivers or lakes or along the coast, under way or not. No search warrant required.

"Prepare to be boarded!" Came the voice

from the bullhorn. Two of the crew held automatic weapons at the ready, and a third was on the twenty caliber machine gun mounted on a turret at the bow. The officer doing all the shouting recognized them from Avalon, and saw the poles in the holders. "Hey what the heck are you guys doing way out here, fishing?"

"Coming back," said Don.

"Catch anything?"

"Yep," said Kyle and reached into the icebox at the rear of the boat, and deep in the ice were three large mackerel that they'd picked up from a local fisherman just that morning in case something like this happened. Kyle reached in and grabbed one by the tail and held it up with two hands.

"Nice," said the Coastie. "Looks like about a ten pounder."

"Hey, what's up?" said Jack. He was still in Army mode and not afraid to ask a question while under fire. "Why would you want to board us? We're Americans."

"We saw you on radar coming from the lane, and a cargo vessel just left the area. For all we knew, you could have been a smuggler."

They all laughed, including the crew on the coast guard ship.

"We heard that's where the fish were running."

The officer nodded his head, and rubbed his chin with indecision.

"Just be careful, it's not advisable to go fishing in that area, especially on a moonless night. You guys should know better. Those cargo ships will run you down."

Then he waved them off and they went back on patrol, the large cutter rumbling out of sight into the black night.

"They saw us on radar," said Jack. "We can't let that happen again."

They found the catamaran at an auction in San Diego, bought it with the money they'd made from the three runs with the rented boat.

They dry docked it, retrofitted it with a carbon fiber Kevlar mast and laid Kevlar matting on the hull and every metal piece on the boat, then tested it out with a buddy of Jack's who had a big fishing boat with a radar bank on the flybridge. The radar signature was clear, a big fat zero and they were back in business.

Kyle loved the Black Cat. In a way it had become his boat over the years and he took care of it like a baby, he paid his dues taking charge of all the maintenance, and he'd paid the other's their fair share of the money they put into it. Another year or two, and they'd be done with the smuggling business, and he'd take the cat around the world and visit any port that he wanted.

He hummed a little tune as he climbed to the top of the mast.

19.

The sun was well behind the island, setting towards the west. The shadows on the harbor were getting deeper and darker. I walked towards the center of town to find a restaurant for dinner.

There was no shortage of bars and restaurants, and shops with knick-knacks and snacks. I meandered along the boardwalk with all the other tourists.

It was mixture of smells and sounds, hot pretzels and salt water taffy and grilled meats mixed with the scent of sand seaweed and ocean, marimba music to the left, jazz to the right and up ahead somewhere in the distance a drummer in a rock band was deep in a solo. A departing ship gave a blast of its foghorn as it headed out to sea.

Lights along the avenues were warming up with a soft glow, a slight mist was forming along the coast as the temperature dropped.

The Coast Guard cutter was tied up at the end of the long green pier. Men were moving about on the deck tying and lashing and coiling ropes. I could see Lieutenant Myles Johnson standing tall in his starched khakis, giving orders.

I decided to take a walk over and say hello, and headed down the pier.

"Permission to come aboard."

He turned and recognized me.

"I'll come down," he shouted. He walked down the gangplank and shook my hand.

"How are you doing Badger?"

"Nice boat."

"It's okay in a pinch, I guess. Good enough for government work."

I knew for a fact that this boat could do forty-five knots on a rough sea.

"I wouldn't want to have to outrun you."

"You'd be surprised how many try."

"Anyone succeed?"

He shook his head. "Not exactly. But there were these guys a couple of months ago. Drug smugglers from Mexico, three in the morning, no moon, got to within twenty miles of Long Beach, running a cigarette boat all juiced up. This boat was all rail and engine if you know what I mean, built to go straight and fast. We were too far away and couldn't make enough headway to catch them before they were gonna get to the coast, so we called in our helicopter and they convinced them to stop."

"Convinced them?"

He smiled. "A couple of twenty-caliber machine gun rounds over the bow is a great negotiating tool. So how is your fiancé Amber doing? I remember she was a little shook up with the body and all."

"Thanks for asking, she's okay. Back at work delivering babies at the hospital. I took her home and decided to come back over."

"Work or pleasure?"

"Neither."

"What else is there?"

"Something in-between. A need to know. I wanted to find out if anyone claimed the body, and they wouldn't tell me over the phone so I took a ride over. I feel somehow responsible to see that she's taken care of."

"I wouldn't know the answer to that. Once we turned her over to the LAPD here on Avalon, it's their case. We move onto other things."

"I went to the morgue. She's still here."

He shook his head. "That's a shame."

"You told me something like this happened before."

"Sure, a couple of years ago, at the beginning of my tour here on Catalina."

"So you wouldn't know if anyone ever claimed the body."

"Nope."

"Did they have a bag of money, and a California driver's license?"

He nodded.

"Do you remember the address on the ID?"

"That was two years ago."

"Bayshore drive?"

His mood changed quickly, I could see it in his eyes.

"I went there to check on Mei Ling," I said. "She never lived there. The ID was a fake. I'm wondering if the two incidents are related."

"Sounds to me like you're conducting an investigation."

"Just a concerned citizen."

"Does the Avalon police department know your concerns?"

"I just came from there. I talked to the deputy Chief, Don Wilson, he took a close look while I was there and confirmed that the driver's license is forged. They're sending the wad of money to the mainland for testing to see if it's fake too."

I didn't tell him that I had to prod Don into taking a closer look at the driver's license.

"What are your plans now?"

"I don't know, I'm here so I might as well hang out for a while, get a feel for the place. I've met some interesting people."

"There's a lot of characters here. Did you sail over?"

"The Sugar? No, I left her in Dana Point, and brought over the Spice. She's right over there, third row, fifth over."

He followed my pointed finger and whistled.

"Very nice. So you have a power boat and a sailboat? Impressive."

I nodded. "Got to cover the bases."

He smiled and reached out to shake my hand again. "Well, nice talking with you Badger, I have to get back up on deck, we're going out on patrol pretty soon."

I wasn't finished with him.

"That body you found, two years ago. The one you told me about. Did you bring it here to Avalon, and turn it over to the police?"

He nodded and bit his lower lip.

"And they probably never told you if it was ever claimed by anyone."

He shook his head. "No, but I'll bet there's a way to find out. You gonna do some more digging?"

"Someone has to."

"You know Badger, I always say it's best to let the pros do what they're trained to do. Let the authorities handle it."

"They're not doing such a great job."

"Give them some time, it's only been two days."

"Maybe I'm impatient."

"Well don't be. There's systems and procedures, and laws that have to be followed. I don't want you to get into trouble, get in over your head. Digging around for answers is fine most of the time unless there's a crime involved, which in this case there very well might be. I just don't want you digging so deep that you dig own grave."

"Thanks for the warning, but I can handle myself."

"I'll bet you can. And it's not a warning. It's just some friendly advice."

"So if it's friendly advice, then why do you say digging for answers might be digging my grave?"

"Because I'd almost forgotten something."

"What."

"The people who found the body two years ago. The old couple from Newport."

"Yeah?"

"They disappeared about a week later. Fell off their boat mid channel. We found it floating, abandoned with the throttle on full and the gas tank empty. It was a windy day and the whitecaps were running high. We figured they hit a rogue wave and got knocked off, and the boat just kept on going without them, round and round in circles till it ran out of gas."

I shook my head in remorse. "They should have been wearing their safety lines."

"One guy falling off his boat without a safety line and having it motor off without him is fairly common. Happens more often than you'd believe. Two people at the same time is, well, a little suspicious."

"You think someone pushed them off?"

"I'm saying we never found any evidence of a struggle, and that it's an unsolved mystery. The only link we have so far is the two bodies, the location where they were found, and the similar type of life jacket."

I studied his face for a moment and couldn't see the slightest hint of a lie.

"Thanks again for the advice. One more thing though. Where's a good place to have dinner?"

He pointed down the avenue. "The Bent Whistle."

20.

I was lounging on the couch next to the railing on the Spice, taking in the scene.

The food at the Bent Whistle was good. Their specialty was buffalo steak, but I went with the fresh halibut steak and potatoes.

The water in the harbor was calm and serene with the lights from shore playing on the surface, and yet small waves slapped against the hull and the Spice gently rocked from a wake as another transfer ferry went by, taking a transient sailor from the shore back to their ship for the evening. Ten-thirty at night and the town was winding down, the restaurants and bars were still bustling, but more and more of the overnight boaters were returning to their cabins to be gently rocked to sleep.

My cell phone lit up and rang, it was Amber.

"Hey sweetie," I said. "How are you doing?"

"Just got off my shift, my feet are tired, but otherwise I just miss you. Where are you?"

"Sitting on the deck of the Spice in Avalon Bay, watching the harbor lights, wishing you were here with me."

"Stop it Badger."

"Sorry, I was just being honest. How was your shift? I hope it was completely and utterly boring."

"Well it was long and not exactly boring. They put me in the maternity ward and we delivered six babies over ten hours. It was like a production line. Four girls and two boys."

I whistled. "Now that's the kind of odds us guys like, two girls for every boy."

"Three normal births, two cesareans, and one elevator."

My face went slack. "A what? I know what a cesarean is, but what the heck is an elevator birth, the kind where you press the belly button and the baby just drops out?"

She giggled. "You know that elevator they've been having trouble with?"

"Yeah."

"Well a woman that was in labor got rushed to the hospital by her husband and they were in such a rush, they didn't see the out of order sign. They got into the bad elevator to go up to the maternity ward, and got stuck between floors. We couldn't get her out in time. There was a four-foot space on the top and a three-foot space on the bottom, but she was too big and in too much pain to squeeze out."

"Holy cow."

"Yeah, holy cow is right, it was crazy. So the maintenance guys forced open the doors, put a ladder up to the opening and Doctor Johnson, Marlene, and I squeezed into the little elevator with blankets and forceps and help this poor woman give birth to a healthy baby boy. Both floors were cheering when they heard the baby cry out."

"That's a good story for the family to tell over the years."

"Yes, but it's a black eye for the hospital. She was in labor for three hours in a stuck elevator, and two news crews showed up to cover the story."

"Ouch. But look on the bright side, it could have been worse, what if an old guy was having a heart attack, got stuck and died."

There was silence as she digested what I said.

"You always have a way of looking at the other side of things, don't you?"

It was true, I always looked on the bad side, it was my nature, thinking about what terrible things could happen and making contingency plans to prevent disaster. It was a constant, continual way of thinking. Sort of like background noise and barely noticeable until someone pointed it out to you. Like if you're sitting in a park enjoying the view, watching the clouds go by and someone sitting next to you would say:

"Do you hear those bees in the tree over there?"

And you would shake your head no, and then listen very carefully to the distant tiny sound and say, "Why yes I do hear them now, I never even noticed..."

Even right now, sitting on my yacht in the

middle of a nice gentle harbor, while watching the transfer ferry go by I studied the people on board, looked for trouble, or a weapon, the barrel of a gun pointed my way, someone getting ready to toss a grenade, in the back of my mind thinking what I would do if someone unloaded a clip at me, how I would dive onto the deck or over the side to escape.

It wasn't post-traumatic stress disorder and I wasn't paranoid. I was an ex-combat trained Marine soldier, had seen some action in the field and some things never really wore off.

I shrugged my shoulders. It was part of my DNA now and there was no sense fighting it. I enjoyed being on the lookout, and wasn't going to let anyone get the jump on me, or anyone I was protecting.

"So when are you coming home?" she asked.

"I don't know. I've got a few more things to check out tomorrow, and then I'll probably head back to Dana Point tomorrow night or the next morning."

I didn't tell her about visiting the morgue and finding out the body was still there and unclaimed, and just left it at that. I wanted to check out a few more things, that's all. I didn't want her worrying about me.

"You're just looking around?"

"Yeah, no big deal, just poking around, seeing what's happening around town. Maybe we'll buy a place, and move here someday."

"Did anyone claim that girl's body yet?"

Busted.

"Not yet."

"That's strange."

"It's not normal. But remember what Lieutenant Myles Johnson said. It happened a few years ago."

"I wish you would just let the authorities take care of it."

"I am. I'm not getting in their way, in fact I think I helped them today."

"How?"

"I had a short meeting with the Deputy Police Chief and helped him with some loose ends. I'll probably meet with him again tomorrow, and then I'll be coming home."

I didn't mention the people who found the guy two years ago disappearing off their boat mid-channel.

"Well," she said. "Just be careful."

I laughed. "Me, careful? Naw..."

"Badger I'll punch you."

"I'm joking Amber, I won't get into any trouble, scout's honor, don't worry." Famous last words. Don't worry. I regretted saying them and knocked my knuckles on my head, and then on the wooden railing for good measure. I could hear her sighing over the line, knowing what I'd just done.

"Call me tomorrow morning," she said. "I'm going to bed now." And she hung up.

I fiddled with my pencil and the drawing on the yellow legal pad on my lap. It was a map of sorts, boxes with the names of the characters on the island, and the mainland, and in China, linked together by lines. Somehow it was all connected, and I studied the links and wondered how.

Jack was a suspect, and Don, but who else? And how did they smuggle the people? What boat did they use?

The silence was broken by three instant and simultaneous events, a high piercing whistle, a cracking sound, and splinters from the railing hitting me in the cheek. I rolled off the couch flat on the deck and stayed down and still, with my heart beating fast. I've heard that whistling sound before, in combat. The whistling sound was a bullet cracking into the railing and sending splinters flying my way.

Someone just took a shot at me.

And missed.

I needed answers, quick. Keeping my head down, I reached over the railing with the pencil and with my finger found the hole from the bullet and put the pencil straight into it, then reached up to the console and grabbed the binoculars and set them to infrared, pulled my black cap over my head, set the binoculars on the edge of the rail and trained them along the line where the pencil was pointing. The bullet's trajectory line. The boat was turning a bit in the wind but not very fast. I had my general target area.

A dark knoll, high above the harbor a mile from the city where a road ran along the cliff. I knew the place. Chimes Tower Road, and the scenic lookout by the Zane house. The road was empty, and yet a vehicle was parked to the side. Someone jumped into it and drove away, down the hill along the winding road towards

Avalon.

I followed its path, and I could see it's outline just for a moment before it disappeared behind some trees. It was a truck, I couldn't tell what color, but it definitely had the shape of a truck with a rack above the bed and something that looked like a stack of lumber or a door. Maybe it was one of the contractors on the island. I kept tracking it as it went towards the little town, losing it now and then as it passed behind homes, and picking it back up through spaces between the houses, I could see the glow of the headlights, and not much else. It stopped in the upper right side of the middle of the town, high on the hill in front of a little one story house. It must have turned into a driveway, since the headlights were shining brighter as though they were pointed straight at the harbor. And then the lights went out.

I needed to move fast. I took a last mental snapshot picture of the house from my view on the boat, and calculated the best I could where in the town it was located. I pulled out a map of the city, shined my red penlight on it, and used my finger to trace the route I thought it must have taken. Then I grabbed my weapons, night scope, and dark hoodie, jumped into the skiff, fired up the little two-stroke engine and headed for shore.

I caught up to the ship-to-shore ferry and passed behind and on the right side. While they were heading back to the dock to pick up some more passengers, I was heading straight in to the beach.

The driver looked back at me with a frown as I passed to the starboard side of their boat. He motioned with his hand in a flat palm downward motion for me to slow down.

I ignored him and cranked the throttle and sped up. Give me a ticket, harbor cop.

Within a few short minutes I shut the engine off, pulled the prop up out of the water to a forty-five degree angle and locked it off. I glided onto the shore, jumped out, and dragged the skiff up past the high water line.

The tide was going out and I knew it would be safe leaving it here for a while. I threw the anchor on the sand by the wall with ten feet of line, to be on the safe side, and headed to the stairway and up to the sidewalk.

No one talked to me or looked sideways as I made my way up onto the walkway that bordered the harbor. One old guy with a half-grey beard looked as though he wanted to say something about my skiff, then thought better when he saw the look in my eyes. He could tell I was in a hurry and was not to be disturbed.

Three streets over I took a left at the Italian Restaurant and took the same route as when I walked to the Zane Grey house for the party with Gale. I headed up the hill past the tidy little yards and quaint little homes of Santa Catalina to a snipers den.

The road angled to the left and about a hundred fifty yards up I took the first right onto the next road and headed a few doors over. This is the spot that I fingered on the map, and sure enough, there was a brand new black truck parked in front of a little house. There were racks above the truck bed, they didn't hold lumber or a door, but a long yellow paddle board.

This is the truck I watched a drunk Corbin get into a few nights ago after beating the hell out of the guy who bested him at a poker game. We were, at the most, two blocks over from the Zane Grey house. I had no idea if Corbin was the same guy who drove this truck tonight, or even if this was his home, but if it was, he was a lazy bastard.

I walked past the house on the opposite side of the street, minding my own business, humming a little tune, just a tourist out for a walk, happy to be on vacation in Avalon.

I went up past a bend in the street until I couldn't see the house with the truck anymore. An electric golf cart went whizzing by, a middle-aged couple heading home. They waved as they passed, but I tilted my head to the side so they couldn't see my face while returning their wave, then walked slowly back the way I'd come, now on the same side of the street that the house was on.

The home was dimly lit and the front door was shut. Trash cans by the left side, a large round bush on the right. I took a quick three-sixty turn to take in my surroundings, looking up at the stars, and then slipped into the driveway and crouched in front of the truck, putting my hand on the hood.

It was very warm. Someone just got home from a drive. Still crouching, I made my way around the right side of the home. Blocked from the street by the large round bush, I looked down the side of the house towards the side window. Here at the corner of the house the electric main breaker and the wire from the street went straight over my head.

There was a drape with a crack in the middle of the window. I crept slowly forward, pressed my nose against the screen, and peered in. It was a dark living room, the light in the hallway was on, and then it too went off, leaving the whole house pitch black. I backed quickly away from the window and pressed into the side of the house. My breathing quickened. I needed to settle it down and get control. Had someone just seen me at the window and was getting ready to blast me?

The front door slammed shut.

Or maybe whoever was inside, saw me and was heading out to confront me face to face. I reached behind my back and slid one of the pistols out of the holster, clicked the safety off, held it with both hands in front of me and got ready for someone to come barging around the corner with a gun.

The truck door slammed shut and the engine started. I raced to the front corner and slithered along the ground and lay under the large bush and waited. I was looking through the branches directly at the passenger side window of the truck, but it was tinted, making the shape of the head inside nearly invisible. It backed out of the little driveway into the street, and when the front tires turned and the truck pivoted onto the road, the streetlight shined straight down through the windshield from above. I could see a large head with slick jet black hair and a overly tanned face.

Corbin.

The truck headed off down the street and took a left headed for the harbor and the middle of the town.

I pulled my hoodie over the top of my head and my cheeks, slid on the mirrored glasses and headed back to the side of the house. I pulled open the main breaker and zapped it with my hand held taser with a loud pop and a crackle. Then I headed to the side window, took off the outside screen and was ready to punch the window, but checked first, and found it was unlocked. I slid the window up and crawled up and into the house next to a couch. I was only looking for one thing, and it didn't take long. Set in a side closet was a long leather case and inside was a long rifle. A sniper's special with a large night scope. I felt the barrel, the cold hard steel was anything but, it was still warm.

When I was in the Army I knew some snipers who would wait twenty minutes between shots to let their barrel cool all the way down to get what they called a cold shot. I figured it had taken me ten minutes at most to get here. This gun had been very recently fired.

I considered removing the firing pin, but that would take too long, maybe two minutes and I didn't want to stay in the house that long.

So I pulled the rifle all the way out of its

case, lodged the tip of the barrel into a door jamb, held the bottom of the door with my foot wedged against it and bent the barrel very slightly. It wasn't much of a bend and the gun would definitely still fire, but at a long distance would lose a lot of accuracy. It wouldn't hit the broadside of a barn from half a mile and was effectively disabled.

After replacing the rifle in its case and putting it back in the exact spot where it was, I took a quick tour of the house to see who I was up against.

Shotgun under the bed, next to the door leading to the bedroom, next to the front door. This guy was just like Jack Wilson, ready to action and maybe a little paranoid. The kitchen was stocked with a lot of booze, whiskeys and beers, muscle building powders, vials of anabolic steroids in the refrigerator. All the ingredients that added up to a volatile attitude.

I sensed that my three minutes was up, and headed back and out through the window, carefully replaced the screen and crept out to the bush. When the coast looked clear I took off my shades, pushed the hoodie off my head, and walked out onto the street. I headed the way the truck went, whistling a tune. Maybe I'd get lucky and see it parked along the way.

I turned left and headed down the hill to the harbor. I'd only travelled about a hundred feet, and halfway down the street when, what do you know, there was the black truck with the yellow surfboard on the rack over the bed. It was parked in a narrow driveway in front of a tiny one-story red-bricked Spanish style house. That lazy bastard drove his truck all of two hundred feet.

There were two other vehicles parked alongside it, a four seat electric golf cart and a white SUV with blue lights on the roof. The County of Los Angeles insignia on the side and in bold letters the words SHERIFF.

This street was well lit, the square homes were packed tight together and it didn't look like there was any way I could sneak along the side and peek in a window. I turned around, tilted my head away from the house and went back up the street to think.

I walked as slow as could without drawing attention to myself. Again I was a carefree tourist just out for a nighttime walk around Avalon. Just passing the time. Not a threat.

Three doors up from the house was a large empty lot that looked like it might do the trick. I could disappear into it, walk along the backyards of the two adjoining houses, and come around the back of the Spanish style house. I walked to the far right corner, did a three-sixty looking up at the sky and the stars and the surrounding buildings. Seeing no prying eyes, I sauntered to the back of the lot and dis-appeared into the dark.

21.

Corbin, Jack Wilson and Don sat around the table, each man with a cup of coffee in front of him.

"Our next shipment was supposed to be next month, what happened?"

"I don't know, all I do know is I got the call this morning and here I am. It's a special order. What do we care? The money's right."

"No drugs," said Don.

"They know that."

"I don't like the fact that we're going out to the lane with that bastard poking around."

"I'm telling you I took care of the problem," said Corbin.

"Taking a shot at someone from half a mile away doesn't take care of the problem," said Don. "It creates a problem. It was a damned stupid thing to do. Someone could have seen you, and then I have to get involved."

"I think I got him. The bullet hit right by his head and he fell onto the deck, I saw the impact. It was a clean shot. He never got back up."

"I hope you're right," said Jack. "I thought when I sank his boat he'd stop sniffing around, and here he is in Avalon. Maybe we should send someone out there to check on him. Make sure he's dead, or incapacitated. And if not, finish the job. Anybody make a report to the police, Don?"

He shook his head. "A couple of people reported hearing what they thought was a gunshot, someone called and complained about firecrackers on the hill, that's all. No gunshot wounds at the hospital, or new bodies at the morgue. Yet. This guy Badger's turning out to be a real pest, went to the mortuary this morning, and then spent half an hour interrogating me in my office."

"Supposed to be the other way around," said Corbin with a sneer. "What kind of cop are you anyways?"

"I'm pretty sure he's the guy who broke into my house yesterday," said Jack. "That guy's got a lot of balls, and I'm gonna bust 'em."

"What about the drop tonight?" asked Don. "Maybe we should call it off."

"What the hell do you mean call it off? We can't call it off."

"I don't like it. What if he follows us to the shipping lane? Calls the Coast Guard and we get stopped and searched?"

"You sank his other boat, right? Let's go out there and sink this one. If he's still on it with a bullet in his head, so much the better."

"It's not that hard, to bust a pipe. We could

stop there on our way to the Black Cat."

"How much time do we have?"

"It's eleven o'clock, so about an hour until we need to be at the boat. We leave at midnight and it's two hours to the drop zone. We should probably get out to the boat pretty soon. What the hell is that?"

They all looked at Corbin, who was holding a small square black shiny object that fit in the palm of his hand.

"A taser. Haven't you ever seen one?"

"Of course I've seen one, I have a whole arsenal at the precinct. I mean what the hell is it doing in your hand."

Corbin pressed the trigger and smiled at the electric bolt crackling between the poles. "It's my new toy, I'm bringing it with me to the lane."

The statement brought an angry exchange with Don.

"The hell you are."

"The hell I'm not."

"Why for God's sake do you want that on the boat? Those things are more dangerous than a gun in the wrong hands."

"If one of those damn Chinamen gets stupid and tries to drag me into the water like on our last trip, I'll taser the bastard and drag him by the hair into the boat."

"If he's dragging you into the water, and you're holding onto him with one hand, and the boat with the other, how are you going to grab the taser?"

Corbin narrowed his eyes, the question was

confusing and he needed to come up with an answer quick. "I'll wedge my leg into the railing and then I'll have two hands free."

"I don't like it."

"You don't like a lot of things these days."

"What the hell is that supposed to mean?"

"Enough, you two," said Jack.

"What's that sound? Someone set an alarm on the clock?"

In the background they could hear a tiny beeping sound, not loud at all, just enough volume to wake you up if you were sleeping, like a clock alarm. Beep, beep, beep, beep.

Jack got up and pulled a pistol out of his shoulder holster, and went to the back door and pushed a button on a box on the wall, and the beeping sound went silent. "This is my new toy. I got here early and installed a few motion detecting sensors around the perimeter. Someone's out there."

"It's probably just a dog or a cat prowling around."

"Or maybe it's our new friend. You want to take that chance?"

Corbin got up, still holding the taser in one hand and picked up a baseball bat that was leaning against the wall with his other hand, gripping it tight. "You two go out the back and I'll circle around from the front, we'll meet in the middle," and he headed to the front door.

22.

The last thing I remembered was the crickets. They were singing in the bushes at the back of the yard by the Spanish style house. I made it through the back yards of the two adjoining houses with no problems.

There were toys to navigate around in the first yard, and gardening supplies in the next, and now it was just gravel, a hedge and the house, and crickets. I remembered how the Indians used the crickets at night when they were hunting. When the crickets were singing, they were happy and safe, and nothing was moving nearby, sentinels of the night, but when they stopped singing, there could be trouble. I remembered they were singing and they were happy and safe, and therefore I was happy and safe, and then for a split second they stopped singing, and I thought they must have sensed my presence and stopped, and so I stopped, and then there was a flash of light in my brain and eyes, shocking pain from head to toe, and then nothing, a void of time, till now.

There were voices nearby, whispering quietly, right above me. It was dark and my head felt like it was split in two, I was face down with my arms pinned under me, I didn't try to move at first, not until I knew where I was, and who was with me.

First my eyes, I fluttered them open, not moving my head. It was dark because there was a rough cloth wrapped around my head. A bandage? I couldn't move my lips, a wide swath of tape held them tight together and I breathed slowly through my nose.

I wriggled my hands ever so slightly. I wasn't pinned, I was bound, zip tied, my legs probably the same. I kept my body still and listened, quieted the pain and fear that gripped me and stayed still with my head angled onto the hard floor where they must have dragged and hog-tied me.

I floated on the edge of consciousness and blinked my eyes to stay awake.

"Now what?"

"I say we shoot him in the head right here and take him out to the lane and dump him."

"Not here, someone will hear the gunshot. Do you have a silencer?"

"Not with me, but I have a couple of pillows, they'll work just as good."

"Not here I said."

"Well it's either here or we drag him out to the lane and do it."

"What if he floats around for a while and some damn pleasure boater finds him? Just like the Chinese girl that got us into this whole damn mess."

"We'll weight him down. Tie a couple of Corbin's barbell plates on him. He'll sink to the bottom like a rock, bottom fish and eels will tear him apart and the crabs will take care of the rest. We get him on the bottom and we're in the clear."

"I didn't get into this for murder."

"Well you're into it now. What other choice do we have?"

"We make this our last run. We're over, we're done with it. I'm done with it. We pump him with drugs till he's passed out and incoherent, dump him on his boat and call the Coast Guard to report a suspected drug dealer. We'll stash coke and meth and some stolen firearms in the hull, get a warrant and find it in the search. He can say anything he wants, no one will ever believe him."

"Where are you gonna get the drugs and guns?"

"Idiot, from the vault at the precinct, I have the key."

"Don't ever call me an idiot again Don, or I'm gonna use this bat on you."

"Framing him for drug running is a gamble, and I don't like gambling. I like guaranteed sure things and the only guaranteed sure thing right now is if we send him to the bottom of the ocean."

"There's no sure thing about a murder either, there's always a loose end somewhere, and there's always someone looking for it. Killing is the real long shot."

"I vote to send him to the bottom."

"I'm a cop, I can't get involved in a murder."

"Cop my ass. You always thought you were better than us, sitting all high and mighty behind your badge. Well I got news for you pal, you're not a cop, you're a criminal like the rest of us. You're just a damned smuggler. You're just as dirty as us. In fact you're more dirty than us. People expect a lot more out of you. They look at me like I'm an alcoholic trouble maker, but you, they look at you like the night in shining armor. You're just a lying piece of shit dirty cop."

"I'm still a cop and I'm done with this business I tell you. All I ever did was bring in some immigrants, I never killed anyone. This is my last run. If you want my help right here and right now, I say we put him on his boat and frame him for drug running and that's it."

"We don't have time for all of that, we have to make the pick-up at the lane in less than three hours."

"We'll bring him with us. Tie him up in one of the holds, and after we drop off the packages at the dock we drop him off on his boat."

"This is getting way too complicated."

"It's the only way I'm going."

"We're running out of time, how are we gonna get him out of here?"

"Wrap him in a blanket, throw him in the back of Corbin's truck."

"Someone's gonna see it and think it's a body."

"That busy body Mrs. Cramer next door."

"We got that roll of artificial turf out back, we'll roll him up in it."

"Looks like he's still out cold, I haven't seen him move a muscle. Man Corbin, you really gave him a wallop."

"Threw the bat as hard as I could like a tomahawk from twenty feet away, hit him right in the side of the head."

"Maybe he's dead and we'll have to go with the first plan after all, and send him to the bottom."

"Kick him and see if he groans."

"I can see his chest moving, he's still breathing."

Someone put a finger on my neck for a moment.

"He's still got a pulse."

"Don, go out to the back yard and get that roll of carpet and let's get going."

Footsteps and a door opening and closing.

Then the voices turned to whispers.

"Look, you and I both know the only sure way to end this guy looking into our business is to get rid of him once and for all. That stupid idea to frame this guy is bullshit. Don's out of it, he's finished. We can't count on him for anything anymore. He's not thinking straight."

"If you ask me, he hasn't been thinking straight for a long time."

"I say we take this guy out to the lane just like Don wants, and then he accidently falls overboard when no one's looking."

"With a sand anchor tied to his feet. We have a fifty pounder on the boat, it'll take about ten seconds to zip tie it on him and toss him over. Whoops."

"Yeah, whoops, and then there's nothing Don can do about it. He's out and we continue to run the business without him. He can't get wise with us because he's an accomplice."

"Here he comes."

The door opened, footsteps dragging something next to me, and then they rolled me over onto a carpet.

"Not too tight," said the voice I recognized as Don's. "We don't want him to suffocate."

They rolled me into the artificial turf and carried me outside and loaded me into the back of the truck. I thought I might have a chance if they put me in the blanket, but now I was like a sardine packed into a can.

We bounced down the hill, around corners and over speed bumps. I could smell the salt air as we got closer to the harbor. Then we stopped, they took me out, and loaded me onto a boat. I could feel the buoyancy of the water, they quickly shoved off and we were heading out to sea, out to the Black Cat and my journey to the bottom with a sand anchor. No one said a word on the short trip, it was getting late, near midnight and the ship-to-shore transfer boats were done for the night. It sounded like we were the only motor on the water. We pulled up next to a boat, I could hear and feel as the sides touched, bumpers squeaking.

"It's about time," said a voice from above.

"We ran into some trouble."

"What the hell is that? Why did you bring a

roll of carpet out here?"

"There's a guy in it."

"What?"

"Long story, help us get this into one of the hulls. He's out like a light."

"It's not gonna fit."

"What are you talking about?"

"It's too long. The roll of carpet is too long to fit."

"You're full of shit."

"I'm telling you it's too long, I know this boat like the back of my hand, and I'm telling you it won't fit through the hatch, it won't bend enough to make the turn."

"I'm gonna give you the back of my hand in a minute."

"Try it, tough guy."

"Okay, it's too long, we're running late as it is. Unroll the guy out of it, and shove him in the hull, how's that?"

"Works for me. Captain?"

"Is this the guy who's been poking his nose where it shouldn't be?"

"One and the same."

"Roll him out and let's have a look. You're sure he's out?"

"Last we checked but you never know, so get ready."

"Naw, leave him in the roll," said the voice from above. "We'll lash him to the deck so we can keep an eye on him. It's safer that way, I don't want him coming to his senses in one of the hulls, he might find a way to do some damage. Or escape."

They lifted me up onto the deck of the boat. I could hear but couldn't feel ropes lashing the roll of carpet that I was trapped inside. I was covered in sweat, or blood, I couldn't tell which, but my entire body felt slick and wet, and I pushed my elbows down by my hips and brought my hands up to the middle of my chest and inched them higher till I was able to tear the duct tape off my lips and took a deep breath. I was completely awake now, and more terrified then before. By twisting my bound hands towards my left shoulder with one elbow up and the other down, there was enough wiggle room to push my arms up and over my head. Stretching up and reaching as high as I could, my fingers grabbed the edge of the end of the roll and I pulled. My body was so slick that I started to move upwards. Keeping as quiet as possible, I used my feet, hands, and elbows to wiggle until my head and shoulders were sticking just a little bit out of the roll. Like a bug coming out of a cocoon.

I was on the deck of the Black Cat, the gloomy sails were unfurled, the lights were out and the entire ship was dark. The four criminals were moving about the ship, tightening lines and getting ready to leave the harbor. I waited for just the right moment, when they were the farthest from where I was stashed, and pulled myself all the way out of the roll and crawled to the edge of railing.

My plan was to slip quietly into the water without a sound, but with my feet and hands bound tight and after being wrapped like a mummy for over an hour, and beaten with a bat, my bones and muscles were stiff as a board. My balance was compromised and I fell rather than slipped into the water with a loud splash.

The water was freezing cold and stunned me. As I took a deep breath and got ready to dive under water I heard someone shout:

"What was that?"

I went straight down, and then angled away from the boat towards what I hoped was towards the shore, but at this point in time the only thing I needed was distance from the Black Cat, in any direction.

Years ago I watched an old video where Jack LaLanne, hands and feet shackled with chains, was able to tow a line of boats full of people through the frigid waters and currents of San Francisco Bay to Alcatraz with a modified dog paddle and frog kick. That's what I used.

Slowly and methodically I swam in a straight line, it felt like I was about six feet under water. I could only hope that it was sweat and not blood that enabled me to wiggle out of the cocoon, or I might soon have company in the water with me. I put that thought out of my mind and glided as far as I could, my breath dwindling, hurting as I held it, one more glide, two more glides and then I was at the danger point of passing out. I slowly rose to the surface, my face rising from the water without a single ripple, quietly pulled in a breath, and then another and another. Nothing sweeter in this world. I'd only travelled about thirty feet but it was enough, it was pitch black on the water, no moon, and they were circling the edge of the boat, all four of them with flashlights pointed down to the water and sweeping the surface.

I slipped under again and kept my pace, modified underwater dog paddle till my breath ran out again and surfaced nearly a hundred feet away. I was halfway to the Spice. Someone from the Black Cat got into the skiff with a flashlight and started circling ever wider around the catamaran while shining the light in the water. I went under water again and dog paddled for my life.

When I came up again the skiff was near the Spice and the guy with the light was shining it up into the cockpit, then he backtracked to the Black Cat, zig-zagging with the light in the water all the way back then gave up and raced back to his boat. The flashlight went off and he tied the skiff to the buoy and climbed aboard the catamaran.

I dog paddled and glided to the back of the Spice then pulled myself up on the transom and crawled into the cockpit. I found my knife in the side by the fighting chair, wedged it between my knees and cut the zip ties on my hands, then with my hands finally free, I used the knife on the zip ties binding my feet.

The only weapon I had on board was this knife and a flare gun, so I opened up a side cabinet marked EMERGENCY and took out the case. This qualified as an emergency in my mind. There was a flare in the chamber and ten others lined up in the case. I patted it and put it on the side.

If they saw me on board and tried to come after me, I could hold them off with a couple of well-placed flares into their skiff, start up my engines, unhook the buoy and outrace any boat on the water.

Except for the Coast Guard interceptor boat, and it wasn't in the harbor at the moment.

I took a deep breath and thought hard. I'd wait here on the Spice till they left the harbor for their little package pickup in the lane. They mentioned two hours to get there. So I'd wait a couple of hours to make sure they made the pickup and I'd call my buddy at the Coast Guard and make sure they were here in the harbor when they returned.

The binoculars were still in the fighting seat where I'd left them after being shot at by Corbin. I picked them up and focused on the Black Cat.

Three of them were lashing down lines on the deck and one of them, who looked like Don, was pointing a pair of binoculars directly at me.

I was still a little woozy and not thinking straight from getting beat up so my head might have been a little bit too high above the railing. I ducked down and cursed.

Ten seconds passed and I crawled farther up inside the cockpit and raised the glasses over the edge again. Now all four of them were standing together, two of them had binoculars and were looking directly at me. One of them pointed. I'd been spotted. I kept my sight on them.

Three of them were having a heated discussion while Don kept his binoculars on me.

No sense in hiding any longer and I stood up straight while keeping the binoculars trained on them. I'd wait for the last moment till they headed my way, and would start my engines.

Three things happened instantaneously.

Two heads semi-exploded. A fragment hit Don and he flinched. Then a third head exploded and Don wheeled around and flew into the water. From my angle I could see the rifle flashes. Two from the left side of the harbor and two from the right. I focused on the left side first. Tucked into the shadows on a flat rock above the water, someone was breaking down and packing a rifle into a case, while on right side a man was still looking through the sight on a long rifle. He was looking towards Don swimming in the water.

He knew he'd missed.

Then he raised the rifle sight until it was pointed directly at me and I ducked behind the railing. He saw me, and he knew that I had seen him. I crawled to the back of the boat, waited ten seconds and raised the binoculars slightly above the rail. He had the rifle broken down and packed, and was moving up from the rock onto the pier. I swung the binoculars back to the left, to the other guy. He was long gone.

The guy on the right was walking quickly, but not too fast as to attract attention. He was tall, that much I could see. There was a cadence and style to his walk. Sharp, crisp, military. He wore a cap and glasses to hide much of his face, but the cheeks, chin, and neck line were visible. Asian. He stopped walking for a moment, pulled out his own pair of binoculars and focused them on me, then swung them to the Black Cat and the figure struggling in the water.

I looked back towards Don. He was in trouble, trying to get back aboard the Black Cat. He was hurt, the assassin must have winged him and that's why he wheeled around and flew into the water, must have gotten him around the shoulder area. He couldn't climb onto the boat and just held on. I looked back towards the Asian assassin, who had disappeared somewhere in the shadows along the pier.

I started the engines, ran to the front and unsnapped the cable holding the boat to the buoy. I slowly idled forward towards the Black Cat while keeping one eye forward and one eye on the pier.

Talk about a gamble; two guys with rifles were running around shooting people and I was heading straight into the scene of the crime. Don saved me, in a way, and I would be damned if I'd let him drown right now. If it wasn't for him I'd probably have a bullet in my head back at their little clubhouse.

I pulled up next to the Black Cat, cut the drive on the engines, and lowered the deck hook into the water.

"Grab onto it," I ordered. I pulled him up

through the marlin gate and sat him down in the cockpit. I could see the other three men spread eagled on the deck of the Black Cat, half their heads missing. Don looked over the railing and could see the same scene as I was looking at. He slumped back and sat down on the deck with his back against the rail and held his right shoulder. His face was ashen, in shock from the shootings, the cold water, the pain and loss of blood.

"How is it, can you tell if it's deep?"

"I got nicked, maybe severed a tendon. I can't use my arm."

"Let's have a look, I don't want you bleeding to death on my boat."

I picked up the knife I'd used to cut my zip tie binds and sliced his shirt open by the shoulder. The wound was bleeding slowly but not profusely. The bullet tore an inch long ridge on the top of his shoulder, nothing that a few stitches couldn't fix. There was a first aid kit in a cabinet within reach. I pulled out a large bandage compress, pressed it tight, and wrapped it with elastic tape.

"Looks like you'll live." He closed his eyes tight and I continued. "If you want to."

"My life is over, I might as well be dead."

"Bullshit," I said. "You're not the one killing people. You're not even going to be a cop anymore, but maybe you still have something to live for, like your wife, for one."

He shook his head and wiped away half a tear. "We all grew up together, since we were little kids running around this harbor. It started out as an easy way to make a little extra money, and then it turned into a lot of money. I guess we got in over our heads. I owe you for pulling me out of the water."

I nodded. "You saved me, and I saved you. We're even."

"Okay."

He had a cop's brain, so I spoke quickly to him. "There were two snipers, one on the left side of the harbor and one on the right, I had a direct line of sight to each of them, they took two shots each, a fragment must have hit you from the first shot, and you moved just enough to make your sniper miss. He saw me with his rifle scope, he knows I saw him, and now he's loose in Avalon. I can't let him get away."

"I can't either. Did you get a good look at them?"

"The guy on the right as he walked down the pier and into the shadows. He looked Asian."

"Coincidence?"

"I guess you could say that."

"Why don't you level with me."

"We must have stepped on the wrong toes."

"We could call the coast guard and your office and get some help."

"The coast guard ship's on the other side of the island. We put out a false alarm to clear them from this area. They're three hours away."

"What about your office, anyone good with a gun?"

"They're best suited for breaking up bar fights and writing tickets for loud behavior and public drunkenness. It'll take too long to get them up to speed." He took a deep breath. "I don't want to get them involved yet."

"Well, they're gonna have to get involved sometime soon, in fact, when it gets light out in couple of hours and people start wondering why a bunch of dead guys are lying around on the Black Cat."

"There's two of them and two of us."

"Where are my handguns?"

"We threw them in the harbor."

I shook my head, what a waste. "We need weapons, nothing long range, this is going to be up close and personal. Let's go to your precinct and pick up a couple of handguns and some shotguns."

"If I show up at the precinct with a bloody shoulder it'll take an hour to explain everything, and there's no way we're gonna catch up to those guys."

"I know a place that has a couple of shotguns and pistols."

"Where?"

"Your buddy Corbin's' house."

"You broke in?"

"He took a shot at me a couple of hours ago."

"Yeah, he told us. He wasn't the brightest guy I've ever known.

"I found his house and looked around a little to see who I was up against. He likes his weapons, and we're gonna put them to use."

"What are you planning?"

"Those two guys who took out your crew?"

"Yeah."

"They're watching us right now."

"How do you know?"

"I just know it, and I also know they're not gonna let you get away. And now I'm involved so they can't let me get away. These guys are contract killers and they don't get paid unless the job is complete, and since I got in the way, I'm on their list. Now, I could just take us out of here, leave the port in my boat right now and head out to sea. There's not a boat in the harbor that could catch us, but that would just be delaying the inevitable. It's either going to be now, or sometime in the future when I have less control, and I'd rather have it be now."

"Yeah."

"There's a couple of different ways this could pan out. They could go into hiding and try to escape the island when the dust clears, they could even be on their way off the island right now. Or, they'll try to finish the job. Tonight." I bit my lip and shook my head. "I think they're going to try to finish it now. Right now. I've seen these kind of guys in action. Once they're hired to do a hit, they have to finish it, or they're the ones that are gonna get hit. They had it all planned out and were ready for you guys. All four of you like sitting ducks on the deck of your boat. Now, how do you suppose they knew you were all going to be in the same place at the same time?"

"We were set up."

"Damned right you were. I know about your Asian connection, the ships from China dropping off human cargo ten miles north of here, I know you were smuggling people. You must have been pretty successful, only losing two in the past couple of years. Why would they want to kill you for that? Rival gang? Whoever set this up knew the exact time you were going to the lane for a pick-up."

"The triad was pressuring us. We didn't... I didn't want to transport drugs. Only people. Maybe they thought they could take over the whole operation, get us all out of the way, and run it the way they wanted to."

"Look," I said. "We could go as far as putting the whole island on alert, turn on the air warning sirens, wake everyone up and tell them to lock their doors and load their guns. Call in the Coast Guard, Air Force, FBI, roll around Avalon in squad cars with bullhorns and tell the assassins to give up."

"And get a lot more people killed."

"Or we take care of it on our own."

He nodded. "Alright."

"This is what's going to happen. We're gonna make it look like we're running for the precinct and the hospital. They're going to try to box us in, up close. But we're not going to the precinct or the hospital. We're going to Corbin's. They'll follow, and we'll have to be ready for them. They'll either be on foot, or steal a car or a golf cart. Either way we just need to make sure we get to our location a few minutes ahead of them. Where's Corbin's truck?"

"By the harbor master's office on the middle pier."

I pulled out the binoculars and searched the pier by the harbor department. There was Corbin's black truck parked next to the building office. It was tucked in and barely visible.

"Where's your car?"

"On the out dock, next to the ferry loading dock. That's where we let off the packages."

"Do you know anyone at the hospital? Or, I should say, do they know you?"

"Of course."

I handed him my cell phone. "Call your office and tell them to bring an ambulance and a squad car out to the dock where your car is parked. Tell them to wait for a ten-foot skiff, we don't want them following us when we make a detour. No sirens, just lights, not a medical emergency, but someone is hurt and needs assistance."

"Why?"

"We need a diversion. We'll head in to the ferry dock and the ambulance, if the assassins are hard pressed to hit us quick, they'll try to ambush us at the dock. They'll get positioned somewhere nearby, out of sight. Right before we get to that pier, we do a one-eighty and gun it for the other pier. It's only a half mile away but we can get there a lot faster than they can if they're on foot. Make the call."

He dialed the phone. "Marilyn, this is Don, we had a little accident out here on Pier One, someone fell and hurt their leg, might be broke. This is not an emergency, I repeat not an emergency, but can you send an ambulance and squad car out here right away? Yep, no sirens, just lights to let everyone know to get out of the way. They'll be coming in on a ten-foot skiff. That's right. Thank you."

He handed the phone back to me and we waited. At midnight on Catalina island you wouldn't expect quick results from emergency responders, but not more than thirty seconds went by and we could see two sets of flashing lights following close behind each other heading, to pier one.

I pushed the throttle forward and started the Spice towards Pier One, engines rumbling, water streaming past the hull.

The squad car and ambulance pulled up next to each other, one person got out of the squad car and two from the ambulance. They waited and watched as we motored straight towards them. Somewhere in the shadows, I was sure, waited two men with long guns.

This is how you get innocent people killed, I thought.

When we were a hundred feet from the dock, I turned the wheel and we headed back out to sea. I pushed the throttle all the way forward. The back of the boat dipped low in the water as the props dug deep with five hundred reps per minute, the bow lifted high in the air. We were up to thirty knots in ten seconds flying over the water towards the pier in the middle of the harbor.

"Get on the port side," I yelled. "And get ready to jump on the dock!"

When we were just fifty feet from the dock,

still doing thirty knots, I pulled the throttle back, let the props set to zero, and pulled into reverse. The boat started bucking and shaking with the torque on the engines and hull. I knew I'd have to have a transmission rebuild at the least, if I lived through this.

We slammed into the dock carrying a five-foot wake with us. It washed over the wood planking and the fiberglass on the side of the boat cracking with the impact. Don jumped out and I threw him the front rope and he held it with his good hand till I jumped out and put a quick two tie on the dock cleat.

We ran to Corbin's truck. He got in the passenger side while I got behind the wheel. He pulled the key from its hiding spot over the visor and I started up the engine and reversed all the way back to the road, with the lights out.

Far on the other side of the harbor I could see two men running fast. I waited for a moment to let them get a little closer so I could get a look. They were tall, wearing dark clothes. I didn't see any long guns. So they must be carrying pistols, all the better.

I reversed all the way out and punched the accelerator to the floorboard. I headed two streets down and took a left, tires squealing, up one street, stopped in front of Corbin's driveway, and backed in. I put it in park and left the engine running, just in case we needed to make a quick getaway.

"We have one, maybe two minutes," I said, and we got out and headed to the front door, each of us carrying a small flashlight. "This is what we'll do. We'll leave the front door open, grab the weapons and come outside and hide on the side of the house under this bush. When they come looking to ambush us inside, that's when we attack."

"I don't have a key to the house," he said.

I ran towards the door, flew both feet in the air, and karate kicked with all my mass at a spot right next to the handle. The door frame splintered as the dead bolt sliced through it and the door slammed against the wall inside the house. I caught myself with my hands on the ground and motioned with my head.

"Let's go."

I went to the living room and grabbed the Glock from the bookcase and a shotgun by the side door. "Can you handle a shotgun with your bad shoulder?" I asked him.

"I wouldn't trust it."

"There's another Glock in the bedroom in the nightstand drawer next to the bed."

He nodded. I went with him and stood at the door, pointing the light next to the bed. My inner clock screamed at me, thirty seconds and we had to get out of there.

He opened the drawer and was about to grab the gun when something bright and flashy caught his eye on the night stand next to the light. He bent to pick something up and sat down heavily on the mattress.

A pair of earrings. Custom, unusual creations. But familiar to him. Large gold hoops with three diamonds on the ends. His head was shaking back and forth as he studied them, turning them over and over in his lap. Then he dropped them both on the ground, picked up the gun from the drawer, and put the barrel next to his temple.

I couldn't watch, and ducked out of the doorframe as the dull thud echoed in the now dark room. I pointed my flashlight back on the lifeless figure sprawled on the bed, dull eyes looking towards the ceiling.

I was stunned for a moment at the sight, and then shook myself out of it.

My inner clock said it was too late to go out the front door, half a minute too late.

I slid over to the side window in the living room and opened it.

I wedged the shotgun through the window and I laid it on the ground outside. I then maneuvered myself out with one hand while holding the Glock with my other.

I see two figures dressed in black walking slowly on the road past the big bush. I move as quickly I could towards it and slid under a branch in the dark shadows. They were each holding a pistol in an upright ready position as they walked towards the house. The streetlight was shining right down on their grim Oriental faces and coal black eyes, oblivious to the fact that they were sitting ducks in the open. If I was closer I could take them both right now.

They fanned out on either side of the truck. They noticed it was still running and looked inside the cab. They gave each other quick hand signals, and the first guy sprinted around the far side of the house while the second guy slid towards the front door.

Half a minute too late.

Unless I can get them positioned together again, my time for ambushing them both has passed.

A tiny pebble moved by my knee, the sound imperceptible, but the guy by the front door heard it and wheeled around with the barrel of a gun. I pull one of the triggers of the double barrel shotgun and he flies backward into the door frame. He gets off a shot that hits the dirt in front of me and raises the gun again. I give him the other barrel and he doubles over and collapses in a heap with a sudden gasp of air leaving his lungs.

Out from under the bush, I drop the shotgun and run to the side of the house. And here comes the other guy, sprinting towards me from the back of the house.

I took quick aim, fired one shot and he hit the deck and rolled away. When I tried to fire again, my pistol jammed. The trigger was stuck and wouldn't budge.

Time to leave.

I turned on my heels and ran back to the front of the house zig-zagging around the corner as bullets whizzed by. I jumped in the truck, put it in drive, and punched the accelerator out of the driveway, burning rubber. I made a right turn, nearly losing control. Out of the corner of my eye I saw a figure leap out the dark onto the back bumper. I zig-zagged the truck with the pedal to the metal hoping he fell off. The speedometer said fifty. There was a sharp corner, so I slowed down while keeping one eye on the rear view mirror. I could see a figure crawl over the back into the bed of the truck, I slammed on the brakes and he barreled into the front of the bed. I punched the accelerator and he slammed into the back of the bed. I came up to another corner. I zig-zagged full speed, grazing the side of a car that was parked on the shoulder. Bullets were flying through the truck cab. The back and front windows exploded, then both side windows. I slammed on the brakes and heard a thud as he hit the front of the bed. I punched the accelerator and the truck was up to fifty again, around the hairpin turn. The Zane Grey house raced past the driver's side. I cranked the wheel back and forth, tires screaming. More bullets flew through the cab, he can't get off a clean shot.

I went straight up Chimes Tower Road to the hairpin turn at the top.

The only glass left in the truck is the rear view mirror. I could see, with one eye, the assassin standing straight up in the bed, wedging his left arm in the strap along the top of the surfboard rack. I viciously cranked the wheel, the truck careening from one side of the road to the other, and slammed on the brakes. But by then his body was secure, his arm wedged tight into the surfboard rack and his feet wedged into the back of the truck bed. As he raised his handgun to take deadly aim at my head, I punch the accelerator, crank the wheel to the right, opened my door, and jump out. I hit the ground on my right side, knocking the wind out of me. I held my arms over my head and rolled thirty miles per hour over rocks and brush tearing at my limbs. I heard a rending crash of metal as the truck jackknifed end over end over the cliff. I stopped rolling, my head face down on a pile of sharp rocks as dust settles around me.

Drifting in and out of consciousness I knew I was hurt badly, I can feel every inch of skin on my body and most of my bones. It was hard to breathe, my lungs were filled with dust and shards of pain.

Blackness covers me. All is quiet and still.

I see Amber. My beautiful Amber. She's walking towards me, her feet gliding on air, dressed all in a white flowing robe. She cradles me in her lap and caresses my head with her fingertips. I see angel wings on her shoulders, all is bright shining gold and light.

Oh my God I'm dead.

She bends down and whispers in my ear. "All will perish, the just and unjust, the righteous and unrighteous, the wicked and the good, all will perish, one and the same. One and the same."

There was the sound of wind in my ears, sirens, and slamming doors. Feet running.

I fell asleep for a moment. Then I woke again, then fell asleep.

I tried to blink my eyes. They're covered in dirt and I can't open them. I try to move my head, my arms, my legs. All over is a sharp and dull overwhelming pain.

I hear a voice shout out. "Here's another one over here!"

Footsteps on gravel, hands turn me slowly over, flashing lights, blue and yellow on the inside of my eyelids. Then gentle fingers on the side of my neck, checking for a pulse.

"This one's still alive."

I tried to open my eyes again but it was useless and I gave up.

This one's still alive, he said.

Meaning the other one was dead.

Pain enveloped my entire being, wrapping me in a searing blanket.

This one's still alive, he said.

For how long, I wondered.

Blackness covered me again.

23.

Mrs. Bailey was in labor for fifteen hours and twenty-five minutes. Her water broke at seven in the morning, her husband dutifully packed her up and brought her to the hospital by eight. She went into labor at ten AM in the maternity ward on the third floor, right at the beginning of Amber's shift.

Everything was going smooth for the first eight hours, a lot of huffing and puffing and pushing and screaming and yelling, and then as her womb was being stretched from the abnormally large child trying to get out of her, she slowly started seeping blood. The huffing and puffing and yelling became more subdued and quiet, and yet the exertion became more intense.

They don't call it labor for nothing. The sheer physical exertion was taking a toll on the poor woman. She was in a fight for her life.

For the first easy eight hours they all joked, doctors, nurses and even the parents, about how a small girl such as herself at all of five-foot zero inches and less than a hundred pounds would fair with a husband as big as a pro wrestler at six-foot eight and three hundred pounds.

One thing was for sure. It was going to be a big child.

The ultrasound looked fine, everything was going well, but time was running against them, and if the large child did not appear soon, they would have to perform an emergency cesarean section. Mrs. Bailey was steadfastly against that, and made it very clear in the beginning that she wanted to forge ahead with a normal childbirth no matter what.

She was nearly fanatical in that desire. But as time wore on, her fanaticism was slowly diminishing.

Her husband held her right hand throughout the entire event. The nurses all took turns holding her left hand as she pushed and yelled, and sometimes screamed out in pain and frustration at the giant head that just would not fit through her small cervix.

In the fourteenth hour she started to get weaker as her blood volume diminished. The blood which was being depleted needed to be replaced.

They put her on an IV drip, yet her blood pressure dipped into a dangerous range. Her body temperature fell, and they wrapped her with extra blankets.

"Don't you leave me," she whispered to her husband through sweat streaked and matted hair that fell onto her face. "You either Amber, please..." she said sweetly to the nurse on her left.

Amber took over holding the left hand two hours ago and even though a couple of times it felt that a bone or two, or at least cartilage might have cracked a few times with the super-human strength in the small woman, she never let go.

Mrs. Bailey took a liking to Amber right off the bat when she first got to the hospital, and told the doctor that no matter how long this took to please keep her by her side. She liked the color of her hair and in between contractions they talked like long lost sisters.

Finally, the crown of the baby's head appeared, a couple of snips of the doctors scissors to make more room, and the baby slid right out into the doctor's waiting hands.

The nurses cleaned up the baby, the doctor did a quick examination with a stethoscope, listening to its heart and breathing and soft crying, put it on a scale, then wrapped it with a soft swaddling blanket. They put a little cloth hat on his head and handed him to his father.

A bouncing baby boy, eleven pounds and eight ounces.

"We should name him Gigantor," joked the father nervously, as he held the baby in his arms. And all the nurses gave him a look, while his wife wiped her face and sighed.

"We'll call him Carl. After my Dad."

The husband was a big tough guy, but he looked utterly and completely terrified to be holding his son. He was afraid to so much as stand up in case he stumbled or passed out and dropped the child. Good thing he was still sitting right next to the bed.

Then he passed the baby very carefully to the mother whose smile filled the room as she finally got a close look at her baby.

"Thank you everyone," she whispered and then turned all her attention to the little package at her breast.

As they all filed out of the room, Amber noted the clock on the wall. One o'clock in the morning. Whew, what a shift. Wait till Badger hears about this one, she thought. He'll get a kick of it, fifteen hours in labor. She smiled at the utter grit and determination of that Mrs. Bailey.

One of the nurses at the main station was on the phone, with a concerned look on her face. When she noticed Amber coming out of Mrs. Baily's room, she motioned her over and pointed to the phone.

"Someone from the police department."

"Hello," said Amber. "Yes, that's me." She listened for a moment to the voice on the other end, then the color left her face, she dropped the phone and fainted straight down into a heap on the floor.

24.

Chang sat quietly in his high backed chair in his unornate office thinking about the consequences of the missed hit in Avalon. It was, after all, only one small aspect of their business and they would survive without it. He tried his best to convince himself that they would carry on without it. He would work it out with the bosses above him and come up with a suitable alternative that would be acceptable to all.

When the assassins did not report in as necessary they knew that something must have gone wrong. The hit was scheduled at midnight and when they did not receive a phone call by dawn of the next morning, it was obvious there would never be a phone call.

And then the police reports filtered in about the shootings on the island. Three well known and local yachtsmen dead on their catamaran, the deputy police chief also shot dead in a private home. Two unidentified Asian men also dead, one shot and the other crushed by a truck that was driven over a cliff. One other man was badly hurt, but was expected to survive.

The FBI was sending a team to the island to help with the investigation, and even Homeland Security was getting involved.

The newspapers were picking up the story and soon the conspiracy theories would swirl for half a day, and then fade away just as quickly as some other tragedy around the world nudged this little story off the front page.

The assassins had failed. Miserably. Still, there was no way they could be traced back to us, Chang thought. They were invisible to the worldwide apparatus that tracked men such as them, no sign of them would show up on any western radar. The FBI would trace their fingerprints and find nothing, for their prints had been altered for just such a scenario.

They had entered the country without going through any official port and, in fact, had arrived on U.S. soil by going through Avalon, picked up by the Black Cat and the Cabal five years ago. It was a strange twist of fate. Five long years ago, and they'd served the Triad very well. Up until now.

The only problem he could sense coming out of this whole mess was the loss of the two assassins. How could they be replaced?

He was so enraptured with trying to decide how they would be able to bring in a new team from China to replace the ones that were lost, that he didn't hear the footsteps behind him. He only turned away from looking out the window when he heard the tiniest of noises like the fluttering of a butterfly's wings. He turned quickly in his chair to see two well-dressed and hardened men flanking the doorway.

Their faces were chiseled from granite, eyes black marbles under brooding eyelids, a calm presence and demeanor that belied an inner volcanic rage that could be unleashed with a spoken word. He knew these men, he had seen them once before when he was summoned to the boss's home long ago. Just prior to being assigned his current position and rank.

Why hadn't his security team alerted him that someone was in the building? That thought faded quickly as he saw the old man standing quietly in the doorframe.

He was thin and ancient, wizened and grey, his long beard and straight hair flowing from his head and face and down to his shoulders like a single hood from a garment. His face, like the chiseled men, was also calm and yet there was not the slightest hint of volcanic rage within these eyes. There was compassion, and a hint of pity and remorse.

He walked slowly into the room, favoring his right leg with a slight limp, and sat in the chair facing the desk.

Chang nearly jumped to his feet when he saw the man and he bowed deeply for a full minute as the old man entered the room and settled into the seat in front of him. He kept standing, waiting for the gesture from the old man for him to also sit down, but that gesture never came, so he remained upright and waited, being studied by the wrinkled eyes.

"We have a problem on Catalina," said the old one.

"Yes. And no. Our men on Catalina are untraceable."

"So you say. And yet the problem has morphed its way onto these very shores and is inching closer to our doorstep."

"I don't understand."

"Of course you don't."

"But, they are untraceable."

"Nothing and no-one is untraceable. Our sources within the CIA tell us that they have been positively identified as Red Army Chinese Nationals..."

"Impossible!" Chang shouted before he could stop himself, and the two bodyguards moved further into the office. Interrupting the old man was a dangerous thing to do, but somehow the angry word just came out. Chang bowed deeply and apologized. The old man continued.

"...they have been identified as Chinese Nationals with links to the Red Army through fingerprint analysis."

"But their prints have been altered..."

"The amazing thing about technology is that it's ever expanding. If there is a problem, someone will always find a way to solve it. The problem in this case is altered fingerprints, and security scientists have been working on a solution for quite some time now."

He leaned closer to the desk

"It was obvious from their initial scan that

your assassins' prints had been altered, so they employed their new technology, their next generation identifier. They linked the broken lines of the prints with computer software and found the army records. From there, the tiny thread has led to our west coast operations, which are too important to jeopardize. It's an ancient Chinese prophesy come to life: 'The thinnest of threads can be fashioned into the most ornate cloak for an emperor, or a death shroud for the same'."

Chang was visibly shaken and tried to maintain his composure while the old man continued.

"I'm only telling you this as a courtesy to your long and faithful service to us."

This was a farewell speech and Chang knew that he would not be asked to sit down again in this lifetime.

"We have a tenuous relationship with the United States government, as you well know. We are always on their radar and are constantly trying to avoid detection. We are tracked and monitored like the Italian mob and yet there is little they can do to thwart our activities as long as we keep them secret. We chip away at the bottom line and stay safe. We trim the tree of financial reward a little bit at a time and stay safe and secure. It is only when we use too big of an axe, try to take too big of a bite, that we get in trouble and the tree falls directly on top of us. That is what has happened on Catalina."

Chang heard a movement and looked at the

doorway. He saw his young handsome assistant standing there in his immaculate pressed powder blue suit. Maybe he is here to save me, thought Chang for a moment and then the moment faded as he saw the look on his face. There was no pity as on the old man's face. There was triumph.

"Four men gunned down on their yacht in the middle of the night in the safest port in the country. The pinnacle of success on the west coast of America is to be anchored in Avalon, not to be murdered in cold blood. Four well-connected and respected men gunned down by your inept assassins. And then they were laid out cold by someone more cunning and able. Their identities and purpose unveiled with the click of a button. And now the eye of the beast has turned towards us in a most intrusive and invasive way. My office this morning was raided by the FBI, my home in the calm and placid heights above Beverly Hills was turned upside down by agents going through my trash cans, my computers confiscated, my wife and visiting grandchildren turned out while they searched every nook and cranny. My castle has been invaded."

Chang's eyes lowered to the desk and filled with tears.

"I hid in the trunk of a car to travel here. You will now ride out in one."

Chang finished the sentence for him in his own mind, "and never to return".

The old man motioned to one of the guards who stepped around the desk and motioned for

Chang to raise his hands. He frisked him for weapons, pulled out a small handgun from his waistband, and laid it on the desk. He nudged Chang in the back with his extended fingers, herding him like cattle out the door.

The young man unbuttoned his coat and sat in the chair behind the desk.

The old man was brief. "The first order of business is the man they call the Badger.

"That's what I was thinking also," said the young man, and he picked up the pistol on the desk and put it carefully in a drawer on the side. "He killed two of our best assassins."

"Yes," said the old man. "Two of our best, who at the same time were trying to kill him. In fact the loss of one of those of assassins will cost us dearly. He was not supposed to be used for something so frivolous. We had other plans for him. Much bigger plans that now need to be put on hold."

He studied the younger man for a reaction, but the young man waited patiently for Kyong to continue. The old man got slowly up from the chair and walked over to look out of the window. He rested a hand on the window sill looking down at the street far below. He could see Chang being ushered into the back seat of the black sedan. "There's an old Chinese saying. If something is not bothering you. Leave it alone."

"Confucius?"

"Me. It's my old saying. And it's enabled me to gain prosperity throughout my life, and I want to use it as a guiding principal in your new capacity as head of this branch of our organization. Badger is not going to cause any more trouble for us. He's a lone wolf, I know his type. They want to be left alone. Why would you want to pull the tail of a lone wolf unless to test its bite. His action against our men was a reaction to a negative force that was brought against him. Why waste additional assets on something that will bring no money to our table? Pride? Revenge? Those reasons are for fools. Plus, and most importantly, he has proven to be a formidable opponent in war, and is best to be avoided. We have nothing to gain from engaging in another battle with him. There's another old saying from a wise Chinese farmer, 'sometimes life is easier if you plow around the stump'."

He turned away from the window and looked directly at the young man.

"We will continue to trim the tree of prosperity a little at a time, and not get so greedy with the ax that the tree falls on us."

The young man nodded. "Yes Uncle."

"There's another matter."

The old man motioned with his hand and another man came through the door and stood in front of the desk. He moved like a cat, eyes steady and unblinking, the tendons in his neck like cords of rope holding the rest of his body in readiness. He was wearing a black suit with a white shirt, loose enough to move quickly, the cuffs just short enough to reveal the edge of Chinese lettering tattooed on the inside of his wrists.

The young man seated at the desk noticed this, and stood, and bowed, while keeping his eyes on the newcomer.

"This is Wang lei. He is your second in command. We are promoting him this very day. You will work closely with him, he will listen to your instructions, and you will take his advice. He is calm and very capable. He runs a very successful restaurant, has shown tenacity in keeping the peace in his neighborhood, and will a great asset to you."

The young man bowed again. "Yes Uncle." Wang lei means rock pile in Chinese and by the look of his new assistant he could pound a solid granite boulder into that pile.

25.

The Spice rocked as gently as a baby's crib at her berth in the harbor, which was a good thing since I was a bruised purple and scraped red throbbing sore from head to toe. The only place on my body that wasn't bruised or scraped was a little spot above my left eye, Amber reached over and lightly kissed the spot and smiled, trying to cheer me up.

Her action brought back in a flash my dream of her as an angel whispering in my ear, and I managed a slight smile through cracked lips. Maybe she really was an angel. I wanted to hug her but I could barely lift my arms.

The doctors were amazed that I had no broken bones, just five broken ribs, but they were mostly cartilage and didn't count, they told me. Sure they didn't, as long as you didn't try to breathe, cough, or laugh, which wasn't going to happen too soon anyways, laughing that was.

They kept me in the hospital for rest of the night after finding me, and all through the morning, until they ran enough tests to determine that there was no internal bleeding. They let me go after lunch the next day.

I had to fight them to get out of there. The doctors were determined that I needed to stay put and not move an inch from the hospital bed.

"We don't know what complications might show in the next few hours. You have a lot of blood vessels all throughout your body and internal organs that have been bruised and are brittle from rolling on rocks at thirty miles an hour. Something could burst or start seeping and you could be in big trouble very quickly."

I wasn't buying it. I needed fresh air more than a safety net. "You can't keep me here against my will," was my reply.

The lead doctor was forthright. "We can if it's in your best interest. If we think by leaving you're in imminent danger, we'll keep you here. Maybe you're just not thinking clearly."

"Try to keep me here and I'll sue you for malpractice."

He frowned and shook his head.

"Cut him loose," he said to the nurse standing nearby, and then to me. "But don't say we didn't warn you."

I hated hospitals and was glad to get the hell out of there. Amber flew over on a chartered helicopter after finding out what happened and helped me get out to the Spice. My beautiful Amber. Funny how I hated hospitals but I sure as heck loved a nurse.

I was stretched out on the lounge chair on

deck in the shade of the awning. I was trying to find a comfortable position a quarter inch at a time. It was impossible so I gave up trying and just took it. My whole body felt like a big sore stubbed toe.

She reached out her hand and tried to find another place that wasn't either bruised or scraped and finally settled on lightly patting me on the top of my head.

"Can I get you anything?" She asked hopefully. "Club soda with lime on ice?" My favorite drink.

I shook my head miserably. "Not today I'm afraid." My go-to beverage of plain soda water and lime over ice wasn't going to cut it for a while, I was afraid. I threw myself out of a truck going about thirty miles an hour on Chimes Tower Road and took a tumble down a rocky hill, and now I was going to have to fall off the wagon for a little while. I hadn't taken a drink of alcohol in over a year, but that was about to change. Lucky thing Gale and her entourage had left behind some of their high class beverages.

"Go downstairs into the galley. There's a bottle of ice-cold champagne in the top of the fridge, and a bottle of brandy in the cabinet. Get the biggest glass you can find, fill a third with the brandy and top it off with the bubbly." I smiled through broken lips at her. "Please."

The view was fine, we were anchored on calm water which was bluer than the sky. The winds were from the east and the bows of all the boats were pointed into it. All the sterns facing west towards the island. The dry desert island. Catalina.

I'd gotten attached to the place, in more ways than one. I grimaced and adjusted my backside, which was attached to a large island side rock just a few hours ago. The lucky rock that stopped my rolling and prevented me from going all the way over the precipice.

The paramedics found me halfway down the cliff still in one piece, while the Chinese assassin was scattered in pieces along with the broken truck all the way to the bottom, part of an arm still wedged in the surfboard racks.

Amber came back up the stairs with a quarter gallon goblet the size of a flower vase that she'd found in one of the cabinets, and dutifully filled as I requested. She added a straw on the side for comfort.

"It looks like you poured the entire bottle," I said.

"You don't have to drink the whole thing."

"What about you?"

"Someone has to be the designated driver."

I smiled. We weren't going anywhere for quite some time. The first sip, ice cold bubbles bit my lips and then went down smooth and soon another and another until the warm glow of the mixture seeped into my inner pores, blotting out the edges of pain and brought a sigh to my lips.

"Wouldn't you be more comfortable in a real bed, like in a hotel room or a hospital?"

"Are you kidding me? This is like a floating palace. I've got everything I need. A comfy chair, a nice view, my best girl."

Her left eyebrow raised a notch. "Best girl?"

"Only girl." My tongue was getting heavy and thick from the beverage. This was a perfect time to get a hug from a beauty, and I reached out circling my hand around her perfect waist and pulled her closer. Then we heard the deep rumbling of a pair of big engines on a powerful boat idling slowly towards us from the open ocean into the harbor.

I recognized the sound.

It was the Coast Guard fast patrol boat. Silver decks and orange trim. Right at this very moment I despised the color combo as it circled around behind our stern and edged closer, getting right into my comfort zone. Blocking my view of the island. Lieutenant Myles Johnson was standing on the bow and shouted out.

"Permission to come aboard?"

This guy's timing was pathetic. I must have been frowning, but I waved him on anyways. "Sure why not," I called out.

His crew put alongside us, two men tender-hooked the Spices' railing and pulled the two boats together until the sides were tight and secure, then Lt. Johnson hopped aboard with a quick salute to me, and shook Amber's hand.

"Ma'am."

Then he took a good look at me and grimaced. "You look like hell."

"Yeah, well you should see the other guy."

"I did see him. He's dead. I heard the

whole story, and that's one of the reasons I'm here."

"Can I get you a drink? She makes a good one. Knock your socks off."

"I'll take a rain check. Mind if I sit down?"

"Are you guys always so damned polite?"

"Comes with the territory."

I motioned to the bench on the side. He took off his cap and settled in.

"You need to put a little less starch in your uniform, Lieutenant. Loosen up a little bit."

He smiled. "Nice boat you have here."

"I'll trade you. Straight up, your piddly little scow for my big shiny sport cruiser, whatdayasay?"

"I don't think the US government would take kindly to that."

I wagged my index finger at him. "You didn't come all the way out here to compliment me on my boat, so why the special visit? C'mon, out with it."

"It's what we call in the military a de-briefing."

"I'm not in the military. Anymore, that is."

"We've got six dead guys spread all over the harbor and half the town. Two assassins from the Chinese mob, and four buddies who were running a little smuggling operation, one of them a deputy police officer who took his own life."

"I know, I was there." I was gloomy with the thought of it.

"There's a high probability that if you didn't show up on Catalina, we'd only have four dead guys and a lingering mystery that we'd probably never be able to solve."

"I was in the wrong place at the right time."

"I'm going to level with you, Badger. This was going to be the smuggler's last run, one way or another. We've known about their operation for quite some time now, and we've been coordinating with the FBI. They were trying to pinpoint the source of the money for the operation, the kingpins, and they finally got the evidence they needed. It was a combination Red Chinese and Triad operation bringing in spies mixed in with regular civilians. So if they got caught if would look like a normal human smuggling ring. I was trying to warn you to stay out of this, when you came to visit me yesterday. I was surprised to see you here on Catalina, and I didn't want you to get in the way. But you sure as hell found a way to get right smack dab in the middle of it."

"I've got a knack for that. Unfortunately."

And I'll be damned if a little hiccup didn't come up and out of my throat from the bubbly.

Amber giggled, and I nodded at the flower vase in my lap. "Champagne. I'm celebrating still being alive."

"More than you realize."

His statement sobered me up a bit, and I took a sip of my drink and focused my eyes on him, waiting for him to continue.

"Those two guys you edged out? Chinese special forces. The FBI, CIA, NSA, you name it. Every government agency on the map has been after them for two years. Couldn't locate them, or put a glove on 'em. But they knew they were here in the country, somewhere, and up to no good. Professional, military grade assassins."

"I thought they were just wanna-be smugglers."

"What I heard is that the Triad's were having a bit of a turf war among themselves, and these guys were brought in to regulate the situation in Los Angeles. Somehow they got the orders to take out our guys here in Avalon."

"Took you by surprise?"

"Completely. We had no clue this was going to happen."

"In the short time I was with him, Don told me a little about their group. They were friends from little kids days. Growing up right here in Avalon Bay." I shook my head in disgust. "Look at how beautiful this place is, are you kidding me? What else do you need? But they got greedy for money, and it destroyed them. Nearly destroyed me, too."

"You did good Badger."

"What about Mei Ling, if that's really her name, did you find out anything about her?" I was still in the middle of it.

He shook his head. "Not yet. She could have been a spy or just your basic normal run of the mill illegal immigrant sneaking into the country. With no fingerprints we'll probably never find out who she was."

"One thing is for sure," I said. "She was in the wrong place at the wrong time."

"Some people are flying in from L.A. right now, they want to see you, and we're supposed to ferry them out to your boat, or bring you to shore, whichever way you prefer."

"I'm not leaving this boat for anybody."

"We'll bring them out here. They should be landing in about twenty minutes."

"Tell them I'm busy."

"These guys are big shots."

"I don't care if it's the President of the United States. Or the Pope flying in from Rome for that matter." I thought twice about that, lifted my cup to the sky and took a sip in honor of the Pope. But I'd even pass on that guy right now.

"It's the head of the CIA. He was in Los Angeles on some other business, and decided to make a special trip out here, just to see you. Seems you made quite an impression with the agency."

"If you couldn't tell, I'm not in the best of moods right now. What in the hell does he want to see me for?"

Lt. Johnson shrugged his shoulders. "I'm just the taxi driver."

I waved him off with the back of my hand. "Not a chance. Tell him to take a hike." I took another sip of my drink.

Amber cozied up next to me and whispered softly in my ear. "C'mon Badge honey, you know that I really don't want you to get involved in any more dangerous business, but it's the head of the CIA. And he's flying out here just to see you. It wouldn't be nice to say no. Besides, he'll probably just come out here anyways, if he wants to."

She was right. They had me trapped. They could board any vessel they wanted to, day or night.

All I wanted to do was sit in my little deck chair, watch the clouds and the color changes on the island, and take an occasional sip as the sun went down. And now I had to consider a Triad bullseye in the middle of my forehead while listening to the head of a spy agency rattle my cage. Guys like that didn't take day trips just to say hello to a small potato like me. Something bigger was in play. My mood of celebration evaporated.

"Maybe they want to offer you a job," said Myles cheerfully.

"Great, that's all I need."

He was joking in his own way, trying to get me to lighten up, but his statement was more true than he realized. They wanted something from me, and were sending their big dog to get it.

At that moment in time it seemed that I was standing in the middle of the proverbial cross-road and could travel any number of ways. Or none at all.

I could sit right down in the middle of the road and refuse to go any further, or I could continue on the straight and narrow path in front of me that I had chosen, with potential disaster on either side, hedging me in. Amber was right, it was a dangerous business to be in. Events out of my control were leading me, prodding me, into action. I was just a basic ordinary bodyguard, protector of the innocent, seeker of the truth, and it wasn't just the booze making me think this way. I knew that everyone has a route to travel and were given certain talents and gifts of life to manage the journey in whatever choice they made. That's what true life was all about, the God given freedom to choose your own way, whether you wanted to or not.

I wondered about the path that I had chosen. Was it straight and true and right, leading me to redemption? Or straight into a pit of destruction?

The path I had chosen.

And then creeping slowly into the back of my mind, I remembered one of my old martial arts teachers. I was young and bullheaded, inflexible and always wanting to do things my way. He could sense that it might be a problem in the future. He was a seventy-year-old Kung Fu master, grizzled and grey with arms and legs like petrified wood, and eyes like cold black steel that never blinked. He sat me down on a split log in our training area, and in a calm, soothing voice, asked me:

"Was it your idea to create all the stars in the universe and did you create this world that we are standing on? With a wave of your hand did you separate the air and the water and the land? Did you shape a single leaf on a single tree, or create an ounce of the air that you are breathing this very moment? Did you grind the sand on all the beaches and command the waves to break upon them? And did you choose the time of day that the sun will rise, and determine with your unbound wisdom the length of the day and of the night? Have you been here forever, and will you be here forever? With a twinkle in your own eye, did you create yourself? No? Then why do you think that you, and you alone are responsible to choose your path? That is arrogance and vanity and conceit, and for fools. Sometimes the one who created the world and everything in it, also creates the path, and the path chooses you."

I looked glumly down at my mug that was now more than half empty, took one last sip, and handed it to Amber with a sigh. I motioned reluctantly towards the bay.

"Please," I asked her.

She was looking at me quizzically, and then nodded her head as she understood what was happening. She reached the mug over the railing and poured the remainder of the drink into the water. I could hear the last of the drops tinkling into the bay.

"Alright Lieutenant," I said. "Bring the big shot out here, and let's hear what he has to say."

The time to celebrate was over.

Made in the USA
San Bernardino, CA
08 August 2017